"Are you two dating?" Nick felt he had to ask. He'd been wondering about it ever since seeing them on Saturday night.

Nick's irritation at his friend inched upward as Jeff chuckled.

"Meagan and I do see each other from time to time." Jeff grinned and then shook his head. "She's like a sister to me, Nick."

Nick didn't realize he'd been holding his breath until he released it. Suddenly, he felt the need to explain his past actions to Jeff. "Did I ever tell you why I stopped seeing Meagan?"

Jeff shook his head. "You didn't have to. I knew she scared you."

"What I felt for her certainly did. I don't think she ever realized it, though."

"No, you hid it pretty well." Jeff took a drink of his coffee before continuing. "You should have told her."

Nick surprised himself by saying, "I didn't have the guts." He rubbed his fingers over his forehead. "Besides, it wouldn't have changed anything. I was too young to handle the depth of my feelings for her, and much too young to realize how special they were."

Jeff nodded. "That's what I thought."

"I've never felt that way about anyone again." Nick got up again and began to pace back and forth in front of the window. While it felt good to tell someone how he felt, he knew he wouldn't go into all the reasons for their breakup with his friend. Meagan was the one he owed an explanation to, and she m—not after all this time. H of his desk. Nick felt the s only it was worse now. He

JANET LEE BARTON and her husband Dan reside in southern Mississippi and feel blessed to have at least one daughter and her family living nearby. Janet loves being able to share her faith and love of the Lord through her writing. She's very happy that the kind of romances the Lord has called her to write can be read by and shared with women of all ages.

Books by Janet Lee Barton

HEARTSONG PRESENTS
HP434—Family Circle
HP532—A Promise Made
HP562—Family Ties
HP623—A Place To Call Home
HP644—Making Amends

Don't miss out on any of our super romances. Write to us at the following address for information on our newest releases and club information.

Heartsong Presents Readers' Service
PO Box 721
Uhrichsville, OH 44683

Or visit www.heartsongpresents.com

Unforgettable

Janet Lee Barton

Heartsong Presents

A note from the Author:
I love to hear from my readers! You may correspond with me by writing:

Janet Lee Barton
Author Relations
PO Box 721
Uhrichsville, OH 44683

ISBN 1-59310-943-1

UNFORGETTABLE

Copyright © 2006 by Janet Lee Barton. All rights reserved. Except for use in any review, the reproduction or utilization of this work in whole or in part in any form by any electronic, mechanical, or other means, now known or hereafter invented, is forbidden without the permission of Heartsong Presents, an imprint of Barbour Publishing, Inc., PO Box 721, Uhrichsville, Ohio 44683.

Scripture taken from the HOLY BIBLE, NEW INTERNATIONAL VERSION®. NIV®. Copyright © 1973, 1978, 1984 by International Bible Society. Used by permission of Zondervan. All rights reserved.

All of the characters and events in this book are fictitious. Any resemblance to actual persons, living or dead, or to actual events is purely coincidental.

Our mission is to publish and distribute inspirational products offering exceptional value and biblical encouragement to the masses.

PRINTED IN THE U.S.A.

prologue

Councilwoman Claudia Melrose looked out over the sea of faces in front of her while the mayor of Magnolia Bay called the emergency town meeting to order. Sitting in her spot at the table in the front of the room, Claudia could see there wasn't an empty chair left. In fact, the last few people who came in were forced to stand. Buoyed by the fact that so many citizens seemed concerned about Magnolia Bay's future, she sent up a silent prayer that the Lord would give her the right words to say to help save this town.

She returned the smiles of her dear, widowed daughter-in-law, Ronni, and her two best friends, Maureen Simmons and Nelda Benson, whom she knew were all praying right along with her that things would go well. As the mayor cleared his throat and began speaking to the audience, Claudia turned her attention to the matter at hand.

"As you all know, our town is on the verge of dying right out from under us," Mayor Marcus Eddington said bluntly. He was known and admired for his straight talk. "We barely have enough tax base to pay for city services. We have to do something."

"We should have welcomed at least one of those casino owners with open arms," a man in the back of the room yelled. "If we had, we wouldn't be having all these problems now."

"I'm sure we could get in on some of that money if we'd let one use our waterfront, even now," former council member George Riley said from the front row.

George always had wanted to get in on the gambling money, but the other council members had voted him down. The city had shown its position by voting him out—and voting Claudia into his spot on the city council—in the last election. Now Claudia prayed that they all were still as steadfast in their support.

"We didn't call this meeting to vote on letting gambling in our city limits again," the mayor said. "It is time we fight back. This meeting has been called to find a way to bring the tourists back into our town. And to that purpose, I'd like to ask council member Claudia Melrose to address you all."

Claudia took a deep breath and stood. "Thank you, Mayor. Actually, I'd like to report on some progress in trying to bring more commerce to Magnolia Bay. Nelda Benson's son Mike and his wife, Alice, have announced plans to open a new seafood restaurant on Bay Drive. Construction has already started. And Maureen Simmons has talked her granddaughter, Meagan Evans, into opening one of her shops here in town."

"Whoopee," George Riley said sarcastically. "*Two* new businesses—we're growing by leaps and bounds, aren't we?"

Claudia looked over at him. "It's a start, George. We *all* need to give our support to these new businesses. We also need to try to find ways to draw tourists and even more commerce into Magnolia Bay—"

"I still say we should have let the casinos come in when they wanted to."

Claudia pulled herself up to her full height of five feet three inches. "And I say that I lost my son because of the influence of casinos in the area. I've seen neighboring towns begin to see the effects of letting them in. Church attendance is down all over the coast. The divorce rate is going up. I'm proud Magnolia Bay had the strength to turn down the casino owners' offers. And, furthermore, I'm going to fight losing this town to them, if it's the last thing I do, George Riley!"

Up until that point the citizens who'd attended the meeting had only clapped politely at her announcement of new businesses opening up. But the mention of her loss had them showing their loyalty to her and there was a sudden wave as they got to their feet and gave her a standing ovation.

Claudia could see the tears in her daughter-in-law's eyes and the pride in Maureen's. She sent up a silent prayer. *Dear Lord, please let this town come back to life. Please guide us in how to help make that happen. In Jesus' name, I pray. Amen.*

one

Meagan adjusted the dress on the mannequin and stood back against the paper-covered window to assess her work. Finally, after months of planning, all that was left to do was to take the paper off the display window, unlock the door to Meagan's Color Cottage on Monday, and her second shop would be open for business.

She smiled, looking at the four mannequins in the window. It hadn't been easy to get the right skin tones, but after consulting with a float builder in nearby New Orleans, Louisiana, and telling him what she wanted, he'd agreed to paint them for her.

Now she had mannequins representing the subtle differences between Spring, Summer, Fall, and Winter coloring. After all, that was what her business was all about—first, helping her client discover the hues that best complemented the unique skin tones God had given her, then, choosing the right shades of clothing, accessories, and cosmetics that enhance her natural outer beauty. Seeing the confidence her clients gained by applying what they learned during a consultation was truly the most rewarding aspect of her business.

Satisfied that everything was just as she'd envisioned it, Meagan sent up a silent prayer of thankfulness before stepping down from the display window and into the reception area.

Her assistant, Veronica Melrose, met her with two cups

of coffee. She handed one to Meagan before dropping down into one of the plush chairs surrounding a small, round coffee table. "I was just going to tell you it was time for a break."

Meagan sank into the chair closest to her and released a tired sigh and an excited chuckle almost at the same time. "I can't believe we're ready, Ronni! All those weeks of hard work, wondering if we were ever going to make our deadline, and now here we are. Meagan's Color Cottage of Magnolia Bay is actually going to open day after tomorrow."

Ronni nodded. "It is hard to believe we're ready to open."

Meagan smiled at her auburn-haired assistant. Although they'd become almost instant friends, she still wasn't sure why Ronni had applied for the job. She could only surmise that it was just a way to fill the lonesome hours of the day since Ronni's husband's death six months ago. She was sure it wasn't for the money. The Melrose family had been one of the first families to settle Magnolia Bay, and Ronni lived with her mother-in-law in one of the huge mansions overlooking the bay. At any rate it didn't matter why. Meagan was just thankful she was here. "Thanks for all the extra hours you put in helping me finish up today, Ronni. I appreciate it more than I can say."

Ronni waved away her thanks with the flick of her hand. "I think I'm as excited as you are. Almost as tired, too. It looks wonderful."

"It does, doesn't it?" Meagan glanced around the shop. Turning the Victorian cottage into both a shop and a place to live had presented a challenge, as she'd wanted to keep it as true to the period as possible. The upstairs had been transformed into a comfortable apartment with the addition of a well-equipped kitchen and modern bathroom. Accessed by either indoor or outdoor staircases, it was already proving to be a very comfortable place to live. And it would be very convenient for when she needed to come back and check on things after she returned to Dallas.

All of the downstairs area housed the shop. Up a step and behind a glass wall from the reception area, in the original wide foyer, were the four-sided mirrored consultation cubicles, where she would try different fabric swatches and cosmetics to find the most complementary colors for her customers' skin tones and features.

The front and rear parlors, dining room, and library had become showrooms, separated as to cool and warm colors associated with the seasons of the year. At the very back of the shop were the stockroom, her small office, a kitchenette, and a lavatory.

Everything was in its place, glass and mirrors gleamed, the hardwood floors and furnishings were polished to a sheen, and the soft-green carpeted areas freshly vacuumed. It looked even better than she'd envisioned it.

Ronni stirred from her seat. "I think I will take off as soon as I finish this coffee, if you're sure everything is done."

Meagan nodded. "I can't think of another thing to do. You go on home—I'm going to be calling it a day in a little while, myself."

She took a sip of the rich coffee, leaned back in her chair, and closed her eyes. Exhaustion was quickly seeping into her every bone. "I wish I could get out of going to this get-together tonight."

"Meagan, you've been working so hard getting your grandmother's home converted into a business and a place to live, trying to help Magnolia Bay. . . You really should relax a little before Monday."

Meagan opened her eyes and grinned at Ronni. "You're right. And I need to be supportive of Alice and Mike's new restaurant as well as the other businesses in town. Besides, Jeff is too good a friend to have me bow out on him at this late date. I'm just tired. A quick shower will revive me, and thanks to you, I can take the whole day off tomorrow."

Ronni smiled as she rose and stretched before picking up her cup and heading for the kitchenette. "I'm glad you aren't backing out of going. It will do you good to get together with some of your old crowd."

"Why don't you come with us?"

"No, thank you. I don't think I'm up to that just yet."

"I understand." Meagan followed slowly, her heart aching for her new friend. She couldn't even imagine losing a husband—did not even want to think about it—but Ronni was living the nightmare. She rinsed out her cup, wondering if the young widow would someday find another love.

When the phone rang, Ronni answered it and called, "Meagan, it's Jeff for you."

She hurried to the office and took the receiver Ronni handed her. "Thanks, Ronni. You have a good weekend, okay?"

Ronni nodded and whispered, "You have a real good time tonight. I'll see you first thing Monday morning."

Meagan nodded her agreement as she sank into her desk chair and spoke into the phone. "Hi, Jeff. What's up?"

"Just called to make sure you get out of there on time tonight. If you aren't finished, I'll help you tomorrow."

"Don't worry, we got everything done. Ronni is on her way home, and I was just going upstairs." She glanced at her watch. "I'll have plenty of time to get ready."

"Good. I was afraid you might back out on me, and that

wouldn't be good for my image."

"That's not something you have to worry about." Meagan smiled to herself as they set a time for him to pick her up then said good-bye. Jeff Morrison was such a dear. He'd always been there when she needed a brotherly shoulder to cry on, or a helping hand. She didn't know what she'd have done without him to help her with the legalities of opening a business in Mississippi. She'd opened her first shop in Texas, but when she decided to open one in her home state, it seemed that no two states did things quite the same way and she'd turned to Jeff.

She pushed herself up out of the chair with determination. She might not be looking forward to tonight, but Jeff was and she wanted him to have a good time. After all he'd done for her the past few months, he deserved it.

Meagan took one more look around her shop before she turned out the lights and locked up. She felt almost giddy with excitement. No matter how many shops she would open, she knew she'd always feel the same way. But this time, it was even more special because it was in her hometown and it was a dream come true to open a shop here. She'd always known exactly what kind of business she wanted to go into, and while she was working to get her degree in business, she'd also trained to become a color consultant. With a modest inheritance from her grandfather Evans, she was able to open up her first shop in Dallas. That her business had become so successful in only a few years still surprised her, and she could only thank the Lord above for her blessings—and pray that her small part in trying to bring business back to the center of Magnolia Bay would help in the way her grandmother had counted on.

Sudden tears formed as she remembered her grandmother, Maureen Simmons. The only thing missing in Meagan's joy was Grammy M. She missed her so much. She'd been the one who had convinced Meagan to come back and open a shop here in her hometown. So badly did Grammy want Magnolia Bay to come back to life, she'd deeded her first home on Bay Drive to Meagan to turn it into Meagan's Color Cottage and to provide an apartment to live in when she was in town. Meagan still couldn't believe that Grammy had passed away almost as soon as she'd agreed to open a shop here. She could only wish she'd done it sooner, but at least Grammy knew it was going to happen. She'd evidently suffered a stroke and passed away in her sleep a month after renovations started on the cottage that had been in her family for years.

Oh, Grammy, I wish you were here. I want so badly to help Magnolia Bay the way you wanted me to. I'm just not sure how much help one little business is going to be, but I'm going to do all I can to help our town come back to life.

Meagan wiped her eyes. Grammy wouldn't want her crying. She'd be telling her to quit moping and get up and get busy. So Meagan blew her nose and nodded as if her sweet grandmother had just admonished her in person.

Hurrying upstairs, she entered her compact kitchen, and as had quickly become habit since moving in, she poured a glass of iced tea and headed through the living room to the small balcony overlooking the bay. She could get to it from both the living room and her bedroom, and she found it hard not to go out first thing in the morning and the last thing at night. The huge live oak at one side of her balcony, and the magnolia tree on the other, made her feel as if she lived in a tree house. Meagan sighed. She did love the view from out here. Late afternoon sunlight glistened on the water, and she could see several sailboats out in the middle of the bay. A slight breeze lifted the hair off her neck, and she began to relax.

Magnolia Bay would always be home. Her uncle still lived here, and although her parents had moved, they were only about an hour away at Hide-a-Way Lake in Carriere, a town much smaller than Magnolia Bay. Meagan was thrilled to be living closer to them again, even if it wouldn't be forever. But with a shop here and the necessity of checking on it, she would be able to spend more time with them than she had in the past few years.

Of course, if the town council's plans to revive her hometown didn't work, Magnolia Bay might one day be smaller than Carriere. It truly was sad that all the casinos along the coast had run many mom-and-pop shops out of business and hurt the small town's tourist trade drastically. She sent up a silent prayer that the council's push to revive the town would work and that tourists looking for the slower pace of the South would seek out Magnolia Bay once more.

Meagan took a deep breath of gulf air and wondered if her parents were back from their trip. They'd offered to stay and help her get the shop ready, but she knew how long they'd looked forward to the cruise they'd planned to celebrate her dad's retirement. She'd insisted they not postpone it, knowing that they would be back in time for the opening.

Reminding herself that Jeff would be there to pick her up soon, she was just going back inside when the phone rang. She grinned at the sound of the voice on the other end of the line. "Mom! I was just thinking about you and Dad. I'm so glad you are back. How was the trip?"

"The cruise was all we'd dreamed and more, honey. We had a wonderful time, but we're glad to be home. How are things there? Did you get everything done? If not, we can come in and help—"

"No, Mom." Meagan stopped the excited flow. "Everything is ready. I'm just glad you had such a great time. I can't wait to hear all about it!"

"Why don't you come and stay the night and spend tomorrow with us? You know how peaceful it is here. It would give you a chance to relax before Monday."

"Oh, Mom, I'd love to, and I will come out tomorrow, but Jeff talked me into going to the grand opening of that new little café on the beach. You know, the Seaside Surf and Turf. It's the one Alice's husband, Mike, is opening. A lot of the old crowd will be there."

"Oh yes. I did hear they were opening up a new restaurant. I'm glad you are going. A night out with all your friends will do you good. Just get here bright and early tomorrow, okay?"

"I will. I'll meet you at church. Guess I'd better go get ready. Give Dad a hug for me. I'll see you in the morning." Meagan hung up and shifted into high gear, hurrying to the shower.

Minutes later, she was standing in front of the mirror twisting her long blond hair into a loose knot on top of her head. One thing being in the business world had taught her was how to get ready in a short amount of time. After applying a minimum amount of base and powder, she dusted a peachy blush over her cheekbones. She used only enough eye makeup to enhance the clear aqua color of her eyes and stood back to inspect her work. She wasn't sure she'd be glamorous enough for Jeff, but it would have to do.

She quickly slipped into a turquoise and green print

sundress with a matching lightweight jacket and was putting on her earrings when the doorbell rang. She slid her feet into her shoes and hurried to open the outside door.

Jeff was leaning against the doorframe, making an obvious point of looking at his watch. At the sight of Meagan, a grin lit his whole face. "I can't believe you are ready! Is that what they taught you in Big D?" He stepped inside. "If so, it was almost worth you being gone."

Meagan playfully punched his shoulder as he laughed, but she couldn't help chuckling when he continued.

"I remember when you used to keep your dates waiting *forever.*"

"Don't remind me. I was always so flustered, the more I hurried, the longer it took."

"It was always worth the wait. You never looked better than right now, though."

Meagan smiled at the compliment. "Thank you, Jeff. I don't know what my ego would do without you."

She picked up her purse, and they headed out the door and down the back staircase. The two of them continued their lighthearted banter all the way to Jeff's car and the few blocks to the restaurant where they were meeting the rest of the group. The closer they got, the quieter Meagan became.

Jeff parked the car at the edge of the highway running along the beach and turned to her. "Meagan, you aren't nervous, are you?"

She realized she'd been chewing her bottom lip, as she always seemed to when she felt a little anxious. It was silly to feel that way now—she'd gone to school with all these people. Still, she felt an apprehension she didn't understand. "I guess I am. It's just that I haven't seen most of these people in several years—I haven't seen some of them since high school."

Jeff came around to help her out of the car and tucked her hand into the crook of his arm. "There is nothing to be nervous about. Everyone is going to be thrilled to see you."

Meagan smiled and tried to shake off the uneasy feeling that tonight wasn't going to go as planned.

The hostess showed them to the large dining room that had been reserved for their group, and they'd no more than entered before Meagan heard her name yelled out.

She'd know that voice anywhere, and she wasn't surprised when she turned to see a short blond making her way toward them. Meagan smiled. Alice Benson had been her best friend in high school. In fact, Meagan had been so swamped with the renovation, preparing her new shop, and keeping in touch with her employees in Dallas that, other than Jeff, Alice was the only one of her old friends she'd been in touch with since she'd been back. And there had been too little time for that.

She returned the other woman's hug and said, "I tried to call you yesterday to let you know I was coming, but you weren't home."

Alice made a face. "Soccer practice for the girls, grocery shopping, school supplies to buy, running errands for Mike—it's a wonder anyone ever catches me at home."

Meagan could see from the happy light in Alice's eyes that she wasn't really complaining. Her twins were adorable. Alice's husband, Mike, came up and suggested they all sit at the same table, and Alice smiled into his eyes as he slid his arm around her.

Meagan couldn't be happier about her friend's obvious contentment, but she was surprised at the sudden longing she felt for the same kind of relationship. Then she reminded herself that she could have the same thing if she agreed to marry Thad. Guilt washed over her. She hadn't thought of him all day. And she hadn't told him about tonight. He deserved much better.

"Everyone is going to be so happy to see you," Alice said, leading the way to their table. "Hey, y'all. . .look who's back in town!"

Meagan forced a smile as she greeted her old friends. In only minutes the chairs around their table were full of people all talking at once, trying to catch up on the last ten years. Soon her smile felt genuine, and she was glad she'd come. Two other couples from their old neighborhood joined them. There was Debbie and her husband, Eric. They'd fought all the way through high school, before finally admitting they loved each other in college. They'd married right after graduation. Eric was in electronics, and Debbie was a teacher. Kay and Denny were both still single. Kay ran a health club over in Gulfport, and Denny was the owner of a new coffee shop near Meagan's Color Cottage. Denny and Eric had been several years ahead of them in school.

Everyone seemed glad to have her back, excited for her business success, and even happier that she'd answered the call to help their hometown.

"But, Meagan, aren't you going to miss all the hustle and bustle of Big D?" Debbie asked. "Magnolia Bay is pretty small. . . ."

The mention of Dallas brought Thad to mind again, and Meagan felt guilty that she hadn't called him before going out tonight. He'd understand—she was sure he would. He was such a wonderful man.

She had met Thad Cameron when she'd hired him to

help her with advertising for her first shop several years ago. The ad campaign he'd come up with was brilliant, and she gave him all the credit for the quick growth of her business. Even more importantly—he was also a wonderful Christian man and as they'd worked together and attended the same church in Dallas, they seemed to ease into a comfortable relationship. Meagan could easily imagine a life with him at some time in the future, but when he'd asked her to marry him right before she left for Magnolia Bay, instead of immediately saying yes, she'd asked him if she could give him her answer after she got the new shop opened. She still wasn't sure why she hadn't accepted his proposal right away when she knew she was going to say yes. Why hadn't she?

"Meagan? I didn't mean to give you a trick question," Debbie said, bringing her thoughts back to the here and now.

Everyone at the table laughed, including Meagan. "I'm sorry. I just lost my train of thought for a moment. It's wonderful being home again. I didn't realize how much I'd missed Magnolia Bay until I got here. As for the hustle and bustle of a busy city, there are a lot of things to see and places to go right here on the coast. Besides, I'll be going home to Dallas, but I'll be back often to check on things here."

She briefly wondered if Thad would be all right with her going back and forth. They'd never discussed it.

"Exactly what is it you do?" Debbie asked, turning the conversation to Meagan's business.

"It's a women's shop, specializing in color consulting. We each have unique skin tones that are complemented by warm or cool colors, and there are subtle differences within the two groups that are named for the four seasons. First, we find the client's skin tone, then take eye and hair color into consideration to find which hues are the most complementary for the coloring God gave her. After that, it's easy to pick out the shades of makeup and clothing that help bring out her natural beauty. We offer clothing, cosmetics, and accessories arranged by color 'seasons' so each woman can easily find the things that will enhance her own special coloring the best."

She looked at Alice's ash blond hair, green eyes, and delicate, rosy skin tone. "With her coloring, Alice is a definite Summer, and she can wear pastels very well."

Alice looked down at her lavender dress and smiled, while Meagan turned her attention to Debbie. "Debbie, you— with your black hair and brown eyes, and that wonderfully deceiving olive skin—have got to be a Cool Winter. You'd look wonderful in black." Meagan didn't want to say that the gold she had on did nothing at all for her.

When Kay asked what colors she should be wearing, the men took up the question, too.

"How would I look in pink, Meagan?" Jeff asked.

And just like old times, Denny joined the teasing. "Should I be wearing this black suit?"

"I think they consider this 'girl talk.' " Meagan laughed and glanced briefly at each man. "Although, I think several of you gentlemen just *might* benefit from my advice."

"All kidding aside," Jeff said, when the round of laughter at the table had subsided, "I think what you do is really wonderful—helping people feel better about themselves."

Sincere murmurs of agreement rose from the group.

"Thanks, everybody," Meagan said with a smile and turned back to the women at the table. "Let's give the men a break and change the subject; but if you ladies would like to come into the shop, I'll give you a free consultation."

The women willingly agreed to turn their attention

to what the men at the table were most interested in at the moment—food and when they were going to eat it. Everyone began to get in line at the buffet bar Mike had set up especially for them, and they helped themselves to the restaurant's huge seafood selection.

Behind her in line, Jeff whispered into her ear, "Feeling better now?"

She turned to smile at him. "I am. Thank you for bringing me. It's good to see everyone."

Between trips to the food bar, a stream of verbal memories flowed.

"Remember when we all started running around together?" Denny asked.

Debbie motioned to Eric and Denny. "I remember you two teasing us mercilessly."

Denny laughed. "Aw, we weren't at bad as Nick."

Suddenly, Meagan knew why she'd dreaded coming tonight. She felt sick to her stomach as she fought all the unwanted memories rising to the surface. *Nick. Nick. Nick.* The name repeated itself over and over, drowning out all conversation around her.

Nick Chambers had been her first love. She'd been devastated when they broke up, and it'd taken all of her college years to finally convince herself that she was over him. Now, just the mention of his name took her back into memories of the past and her first love.

"Meagan?"

It was only hearing her own name being called that brought her around to the present once more. She wasn't sure who had said her name, but thought it was Alice.

"I'm sorry, did you say something?" Meagan asked her friend.

Alice nodded. "I was wondering if you've seen Nick since you've been back. He's really changed a lot over the years."

Meagan shook her head. "I wasn't aware he'd moved back."

"Jeff is a member of his law firm." Alice looked at Jeff. "You didn't tell her?"

Jeff shook his head.

Meagan could only stare at him. Did he really work for Nick? Why hadn't he mentioned it to her? She felt confused, betrayed, and angry.

Jeff must have read the turmoil going on inside her. He touched her shoulder. "Come on, let's go get some dessert."

Meagan knew she couldn't eat a bite, but she wanted the chance to talk to Jeff alone. They'd barely left the table before she turned to him. "Why didn't you tell me?"

"I'm sorry, Meagan. I honestly assumed you knew. The name of the law firm is still Chambers and Associates. I was taking my cue from you. I figured if you were curious about Nick, you'd ask. You never did."

Meagan shrugged and picked up a dessert plate, dishing up first one and then another item without taking note of what she picked. "I thought he was still gone. It never dawned on me that he might have gone into business with his grandfather. I had no idea Nick had moved back and taken over for him."

"I'm sorry." Jeff was filling his plate, too. "It got to be such a habit, staying friends with both of you, that I just didn't mention either of your names to each other."

"And you work for him?"

Jeff nodded. "If it's any consolation to you, he's been out of town a lot, and I don't think he realizes *you* are a client. He's not the boy you knew, Meagan. You knew he lost his mom, but not that his dad died right after Nick graduated from college. His grandparents took in his sister, and Nick went on to law school. The year after he joined the firm, his grandfather died. Now it's just Nick, his sister, and his grandmother."

Tears flooded Meagan's eyes. Nick had certainly suffered more than his share of heartaches. Tori had only been about three when Meagan and Nick were seeing each other in his senior year. There was a big difference in their ages, and she remembered how crazy Nick had been about his baby sister. She blinked quickly, trying to hold her tears at bay. "How old is his sister, now?"

"She'll be sixteen in just a few weeks." Jeff chuckled. "Nick's finding raising a teenager is not a piece of cake."

Meagan couldn't help smiling. If Nick's little sister was anything like he'd been, he probably had his hands full. With their plates loaded with desserts, she and Jeff headed back to the table. As they approached, the conversation stopped suddenly, and she felt all eyes on her.

Meagan looked into the eyes of a small brunette as Alice introduced her as Darla Jenkins. She vaguely remembered Darla as being nice and friendly but not one of the group she ran around with.

"I don't think you need an introduction to her date," Alice continued as Meagan lifted her gaze to the man standing behind Darla.

She felt the color drain from her face. Nick Chambers stood there looking as if he, too, had seen a vision from the past. She caught the angry look he flashed Jeff before his eyes returned to hers.

It really was Nick. A more mature, ruggedly handsome one than she remembered, but definitely Nick. His thick, dark hair was frosted with just a touch of silver at the temples. His eyes were the same warm brown with flecks of gold; only now, there were a few lines around them that told of the passing years.

Meeting Nick's gaze, all those years seemed to fall away, and Meagan felt like a teenager again—and just as vulnerable and confused as she'd been the last time she'd stood this close to him. All the feelings she'd felt then suddenly resurfaced, and she knew that instead of getting rid of them, she'd only buried them somewhere deep inside. Now those same emotions rose up with such force they took her breath away.

two

Wanting nothing more than to turn and run, yet knowing how it would look if they left at that moment, Meagan allowed Jeff to push her gently into her seat. She wouldn't be able to walk across the room, anyway; her legs felt as if they'd suddenly turned to jelly.

Nick sat down in the seat across from her, and Meagan prayed that someone would say something—anything to break the silence. She prayed for the Lord to show her how to handle the situation, but her mind seemed to have gone blank and she was sure no sound could possibly make its way around the knot in her throat.

After what seemed like hours, but in reality could only have been a matter of minutes, the silence was broken.

"It's good to see you, Meagan," Nick said, his voice deeper than she remembered. "What brings you back to town?"

Meagan was saved from answering when Alice volunteered the information. "Meagan is here to help Magnolia Bay by opening a new shop called Meagan's Color Cottage. It opens on Monday."

Nick sent Jeff a sharp look. "I think I've heard that name recently."

Meagan finally managed to swallow around the lump in her throat. She held her head high. "Probably. Your firm is handling all the legal matters for me."

Nick's gaze never left hers. "I don't believe I was told you were the owner."

"And I just learned you now own the law firm I am doing business with." Meagan glanced at Jeff.

"Sometimes, I find it hard to believe *I* am the head of the firm. I have such *capable* people working for me." The look he gave Jeff wasn't lost on Meagan.

Realizing Nick wasn't any more pleased with Jeff than she was gave them a connection that Meagan wasn't sure she wanted. "Sometimes I find it hard to believe I own my own business and that I'm actually opening a second shop in my hometown. I hope it'll be easier after Monday."

"It should be easy now, after all the hours you've been putting in getting everything ready." Jeff chuckled, seemingly unaffected by the discomfort at the table. "I was beginning to think she was going to work right on into Monday without a break," he said to no one in particular. Everyone seemed to be glad for any reason to laugh, and the tension around the table began to subside.

Aware that the reprieve was only temporary for her, Meagan grabbed at the chance to get away from its cause.

"It has been a long day." She picked up her bag and stood. Jeff was at her side at once. "I think I'll call it a night. It was wonderful seeing you all again." *With one exception,* she thought.

She and Jeff made a quick exit after their friends called out a round of best wishes and promises to get together again soon. The short ride home was quiet until Jeff broke the silence.

"Meagan, I really didn't know Nick was going to be there. I would have told you if I'd known."

"It's all right, Jeff. I'd have run into him sooner or later." She rubbed her now throbbing temple. "He really didn't know I was a client, did he?"

Jeff shook his head. "The law firm is growing, but with Magnolia Bay's decline we had to expand our client base, so a lot of our business is out of town. Nick has been traveling more than usual in the last few months. I had mentioned the name of your shop over the phone, but Nick said he knew I could handle everything here, and I didn't think there was really any reason to tell him your name. Or there didn't seem to be at the time." He grinned. "I have a feeling he's going to tell me I thought wrong, though. He's not very happy with me right at this moment."

Jeff pulled up to her shop and came around to open the door for her. Draping his arm casually around her shoulders, he walked Meagan up the outside staircase to her apartment. Taking the keys from her, he unlocked her door before saying, "I really am sorry about the way the night ended, Meagan."

"I know. So am I. You go on back and have a good time."

Jeff chuckled and shook his head. "I think I'll just go on home. I'm not looking forward to that confrontation with Nick. I'll put it off until Monday, if I can." He added, "I know that look. Take something for that headache, get a good night's sleep, and I'll check on you tomorrow."

Meagan didn't have the strength to argue as he pulled the door shut behind him. She made her way into her small kitchen to get some aspirin, hoping the pills would ease her pounding head—and soon. It was just the surprise of seeing Nick after so many years that had sent her into such a tailspin; it couldn't be anything else. She'd been over him for so long she couldn't remember the last time she'd thought of him.

She turned off the lights and went out onto the balcony. As she leaned against the balustrade and looked out over the bay, her thoughts went back over the encounter with Nick. It was so clear, now, why she'd felt apprehensive about going tonight. Consciously, she hadn't given Nick Chambers a thought in years. Now she knew, with a certainty she couldn't explain, that her subconscious had been working overtime on him.

Well, she certainly was making up for all that time now, Meagan realized as she went into her bedroom and got ready for bed automatically. Memories were being released from her subconscious with such fury she didn't have time to settle on just one. They flitted from one to another so fast she felt almost dizzy.

Meagan folded back the covers and turned off her bedside lamp. After saying her prayers, she crawled into bed, closed her eyes tight, and tried to will thoughts of Nick out of her mind. It wasn't easy, but by forcing herself to think about her shop and its opening on Monday, she finally lulled herself into a restless sleep.

❧

Meagan had forgotten to set her alarm and had to hurry to get on the road in time to meet her parents at the country church they attended the next morning. It was on the hour drive that she was finally unable to keep thoughts of Nick at bay any longer. If anything, he'd become even better-looking as an adult. The lines around his eyes gave evidence that the road to manhood hadn't been easy, but they also added character to his face that only made it more attractive.

He'd had a lot to adjust to in his life, and Meagan wondered how much he'd changed because of it. Neither of them were the same two people they'd been ten years ago, yet there'd been a look in Nick's eyes last night that had been so very familiar to her. Again, she found herself wondering why they'd stopped seeing each other. What had happened to make Nick act as if he'd never cared about her? She sighed. Maybe there were no answers.

Meagan shook her head. There was no sense thinking about it now. The years had passed without any answers, and there was no reason to believe she'd get any now. She'd had plenty of practice of blocking out thoughts of Nick, and she did so now as she pulled into the church parking lot.

She hugged both her parents as she slid into the pew beside them only minutes before the service began. They looked wonderful—so tanned, healthy, and happy.

Brad and Jenny Evans were the kind of parents who'd taught her all they could, led her to the Lord, and prepared her, as best they could, for life on her own. They'd always been there when she needed them, and she knew they always would be.

Meagan realized how lucky she was that she still had them and thanked the Lord that she did. Nick had lost so many of those he loved. First his mother, then his dad and grandfather. She hoped there had been someone in his life to help him through those times. Her eyes misted at the thought that he might have had to face them alone.

As the church service got under way and the comfort of it all—the prayers, partaking of the Lord's Supper, the singing, and the wonderful lesson the minister brought to them—eased her mind. When the service was over she hugged her parents again, with an exuberance they returned naturally.

Meagan followed them home in her car, and as she turned onto the road leading to Hide-a-Way Lake, she felt the area's peacefulness close around her. The road curved around homes and lots set among pine, oak, and magnolia trees. Another curve brought the Hide-a-Way Lake Lodge and Restaurant into view. A swimming pool lay at one side of the building; tennis courts and boat docks lay at the other. At the back of the lodge, sand had been hauled in to form a beach on the lake.

It was such an idyllic setting; Meagan understood why her parents had decided to build their retirement home here. The sun glistened brightly on the lake behind the house as Meagan turned into her parents' drive and parked her car under a huge magnolia tree. She hurried around back and up the deck, just as her mother came out with a pitcher of iced tea.

"Thanks, Mom." She took a sip from the glass her mother handed her and plopped down into a deck chair. "I know you saw a lot of beautiful places while you were gone, but I'm sure you can't beat this for tranquility."

They spent the next few hours looking at pictures her parents had taken on their trip, talking about exotic locales and luxurious shipboard life. When conversation drifted to the amount of food they'd been served each day, her dad decided he was starved, and they all headed for the kitchen. After consuming sandwiches even Dagwood would have been proud of, they changed into swimsuits and went back outside to spend the rest of the afternoon swimming, waterskiing, and just soaking up the sun.

Her mother pitched a tube of suntan lotion to her. "Better put some of this on. You are looking a little done around the edges. I don't think you want to look like a boiled lobster tomorrow."

"You don't think my customers would have much faith in me if I told them I was a burnt Spring, huh?" Meagan took her mother's advice and smeared the lotion on.

Her dad chuckled at her remark then said, "Meagan, honey, come rub some of that stuff on my head, would you?"

Meagan went over to him and dropped a kiss on his head before applying a coat to his bald spot. "Dad, why don't you just wear a hat?"

"And have a white bald spot, when the rest of me is so beautifully bronze?"

"I guess you have a point there." Meagan laughed at the thought.

The sun was just beginning to set when they all decided they were getting hungry again. Meagan's dad started the grill while she and her mother took turns getting their showers.

It wasn't until she went to "her" room that thoughts of Nick invaded her mind again. Walking into the room was like walking back in time. Her mother had decorated it with mementos of her high school and college years.

There were posters, pennants, dried corsages, and photo albums scattered here and there. Meagan pulled on her capris and top quickly. Being in the room suddenly made her feel seventeen again, in love with Nick, and devastated by their breakup.

Meagan turned and nearly ran out of the room. She couldn't get away from those memories fast enough and hurried down the stairs. Forcing a smile to her lips, she entered the kitchen.

"Sorry I took so long," she said as she took the lettuce from her mother and began to tear it into pieces for the salad.

Her mother looked at her closely and shrugged her shoulders. "Your dad is watching the steaks, and the potatoes are in the microwave. There isn't anything left to do but make the salad." She took radishes and onions out of the refrigerator and laid them on the counter. "You're looking tired, hon. Did you get too much sun, or do too much reminiscing last night?"

"Probably both," Meagan answered, thinking her mother read her entirely too well.

"Did you have a good time? Your dad and I had a ball last time we got together with some of our old high school group."

"It was all right," Meagan answered as she began slicing the radishes. "Mom, I saw Nick last night."

"Nick Chambers? I thought he'd moved away."

Meagan shook her head. "He lives in Magnolia Bay again. He took over his grandfather's law firm. In fact, Jeff works for him. I didn't know until last night that I'm doing business with Nick's firm."

Her mom started slicing onions. "It was rough, huh?"

Meagan only nodded. She really didn't want to talk about it.

"How is Thad? Have you given him an answer to that proposal yet?"

"He's good." *Last time I talked to him, anyway.* "And no, I haven't given him an answer yet." Meagan knew her mother was only trying to help by changing the subject, but her words only served to remind her that not only had she not told Thad where she was going last night—she hadn't told him where she would be today. And her cell phone was at home. The battery was bad, and she hadn't had time to get a new one for it. If he'd tried to contact her, he was probably getting a little worried by now. Maybe she should call him—

Her dad stuck his head around the door, distracting her.

"Steaks are ready when you are."

As if on cue, the timer went off on the microwave. "We're ready," Meagan's mom said as she put the potatoes in a bowl.

I'll call and apologize when I get home. Meagan gave the salad one more toss, and they headed for the deck.

The steaks were done to perfection, the potatoes soft and fluffy. Neither Nick's nor Thad's names came up again, so the dinner was a relaxing one. Meagan always enjoyed her parents' company. Tonight the conversation centered on the opening of her shop, how it and other new businesses could help Magnolia Bay, and how much the casinos in the area had hurt the town.

"I'm not sure my little shop can help that much. I just hope I'm living up to Grammy's wishes and that I'm doing things the way she would want me to." Meagan expressed her fears.

"Mother was so happy you were opening a shop here. You gave her the peace of mind she needed about her town. She was ready to go, honey. As much as we all miss her, I know she was tremendously proud of you and your willingness to help Magnolia Bay. Needless to say, we're delighted that she talked you into it, too."

"So am I," Meagan assured her mother. They hugged each other then cleared the table and went inside. "Now let me help with the dishes before I go."

"No. There are hardly any to do, and your dad will help me. If you don't go home and get some sleep, you're going to be late for your own opening."

Laughing, Meagan said, "Well, we can't have that." She gathered up her things and her parents walked her to her car.

After giving her a bear hug, her dad whispered, "Don't be

surprised to see me tag along with your mom. I can't let her have all the fun. Besides, it's not every day that a parent gets to watch his child open her own business." Meagan's eyes blurred with tears when he added, "We're awfully proud of you, honey."

She gave him a kiss on the cheek. "I'm the proud one, Dad, that I have you and Mom for parents."

"We'll see you in the morning." Her mother kissed her cheek. "Get a good night's sleep."

Meagan backed out of the driveway as her parents stood, arm in arm, waving good-bye. The drive home seemed longer than usual, making her glad she'd showered at her parents' house. She didn't think she'd be able to stay awake long enough to take one when she got home.

The phone was ringing as she fumbled to unlock her door, but by the time she reached it, whoever it was had given up before her answering machine caught it. But she did have several messages from Thad. She felt awful when she heard his voice saying he was sorry he'd missed her and to call whenever she came in, no matter how late it was. Then another one telling her he was getting a little worried.

Had she always been so inconsiderate of others? Or was it a new trait she was acquiring? Meagan dialed Thad's number on her cordless phone and walked outside onto the balcony.

He picked up on the second ring. "Meagan?"

"Yes, it's me, Thad. I am so sorry I didn't let you know I was going to my parents' for the day."

"It's all right. I was beginning to get a little worried about you, though. I'm just glad you are all right. I've tried since last night, and your cell phone doesn't seem to be working—"

"I have to get a new battery for it. But I should have called you." Meagan felt as if she were drowning in guilt. "I've just been so busy and—"

"I know you have. Don't feel bad. I'm feeling bad enough for both of us that I couldn't get away for your opening."

"I understand, Thad." Looking out across the water at the lights along the other shore, Dallas seemed far away, and suddenly, so did the man who'd asked her to marry him.

"I miss you."

"I miss you, too," Meagan replied honestly. She did miss his company and his quiet support of her and anything she wanted to do. Still, for some reason, she couldn't think of much to say.

"Are you excited about the opening tomorrow?"

That she could talk about. "Oh, yes, I am. The shop is lovely, and I am hoping we have a good turnout."

"I'm sure you will. I just wish I could be there to help you."

"I know you do." And she was sure he did. "How is everything there?"

"It's lonesome with you gone. I went to dinner with Cole Bannister and several others from church tonight. Everyone says to tell you not to get too comfortable back home. They all miss you, too."

Meagan asked about several of their friends from the church they both attended, and they shared a few minutes of small talk before Thad seemed to sense she was getting tired.

"I'd better let you go. You have a big day ahead of you tomorrow."

"I do. I'll let you now how it goes," she promised, stifling a yawn.

"Good. I'll talk to you tomorrow. Sleep well."

"You, too. Good night, Thad." Meagan hung up the

receiver, wondering why she felt so unsettled. She tried to shake off the feeling as she went inside and prepared for bed, telling herself she was just tired and excited about the next day.

It took no more than ten minutes to get ready for bed and set the alarm clock. She said her nightly prayers, tumbled into bed, and fell into a deep, dreamless sleep.

three

Awake long before her alarm clock was set to go off, Meagan said a prayer, once again thanking the Lord for her grandmother's encouragement and generosity in helping make her dream of someday opening her own business in Magnolia Bay come true. She prayed she would be able to live up to Grammy's expectations.

Throwing off the covers, she jumped out of bed feeling almost giddy with excitement. Today was the day. Meagan's Color Cottage of Magnolia Bay was finally going to open for business. Meagan hurried into the kitchen to put the coffee on.

Thirty minutes later, after showering and applying makeup, she began to French braid her hair with fingers that shook nervously. Finally, after the third try, she rolled the loose braid up to the base of her neck and tucked it under, then looked in the mirror to inspect her work. A few tendrils had escaped and now curled around her face, giving her the professional, yet feminine look she'd strived for. She'd decided what to wear, weeks ago, and was pleased with her selection as she dressed in an aqua blouse and ivory silk suit that enhanced the light tan she'd acquired the day before. Matching shoes and gold jewelry were her accessories.

Meagan looked into the mirror and assured herself that the colors she'd chosen brought out her Warm Spring coloring. She was glad she felt good about the way she looked—she needed all the help she could get today.

Her stomach fluttered just thinking about the day ahead, and she decided to make some toast to go with her coffee. Like most people brought up in the South, she liked her coffee strong. She knew from experience, however, that coffee on an empty stomach certainly wasn't going to settle her nerves.

Pulling bread out of her pantry, she was startled by the peal of the upstairs doorbell. She hurried to the door, wondering who could possibly be here this early. *Probably Mom*, she thought as she opened the door. Instead, it was Ronni, standing there with a fast-food bag in her hand. She was a perfect example of Warm Autumn, dressed in a moss green dress that made the most of her auburn hair and hazel eyes.

"I thought you might like a celebration breakfast," Ronni said, holding out the bag. "I brought your favorite sausage biscuits."

"That sounds much better than toast!" Meagan chuckled and pulled her inside. "Pull up a seat, and I'll get you some coffee."

Ronni slid onto one of the stools at the bar separating the kitchen from the dining area while Meagan filled two cups with the fragrant liquid.

"Are you all right?" Ronni asked, a worried frown on her face.

"Of course," Meagan said, unwrapping her breakfast. "Why wouldn't I be?"

Ronni shrugged. "Well, Jeff called me yesterday. He was worried because he couldn't get in touch with you."

Meagan swallowed a bite of biscuit. "I was at my parents' and didn't get back until late."

Ronni nodded. "I told him that's probably where you were." She paused to take a sip of hot coffee. "He told me about Nick Chambers."

The mention of Nick's name made Meagan's heart skip a beat, and she tried to keep her cup from shaking as she raised it to her mouth. "Oh? What did he tell you?"

"Just that you'd gone out with him back in high school, and that you were pretty upset about seeing him the other night."

Meagan shrugged, striving to appear nonchalant. "I was just surprised to see him after all these years; I didn't know he was living here again."

For a moment Meagan thought Ronni was going to ask more about Nick, but she seemed to think better of it and they turned quiet as they finished their breakfast, each busy with her own thoughts.

Meagan's were on Nick once more; she hoped he wouldn't give Jeff too hard a time. She briefly wondered if she would see Nick today. Would he show up at her opening? She sighed and shook her head. Then, with experience born of practice, Meagan put him out of her thoughts. Today wasn't going to be ruined by bittersweet memories; she had too much to be happy about. With a sense of purpose, she gathered up the cups and put them in the kitchen sink, excited anticipation filling her as she looked at the clock. "Come on, Ronni. Let's get this show on the road."

❧

It was getting close to nine when Meagan and Ronni went downstairs to the shop. With little over an hour before opening time, there was much do and they quickly got busy. She opened the front door to the florist from whom she'd ordered an arrangement for the store's opening and was surprised to find the front porch full of early deliveries from several other florists in town. There were floral arrangements of all shapes and sizes, all with notes congratulating her on the opening of Meagan's Color Cottage.

The sweet scent of flowers filled the air as Meagan and Ronni started carrying them inside.

"Oh look," Ronni said, picking up the largest one. "This is from the chamber of commerce; isn't it lovely?"

"It's beautiful. We'd better put it on the table, here in the entry." Meagan was busy bringing in two slightly smaller ones. "Look, Ronni, this one is from Jeff."

Ronni took the card Meagan was holding and read it out loud. "Thought you girls would never make it, but you proved me wrong. Congratulations!"

She took the arrangement from Meagan and buried her nose in the carnations. "Isn't he sweet?"

Meagan laughed. If she didn't know better, she might think Ronni was interested in Jeff. But she knew it was only wishful thinking on her part. Ronni wasn't ready for another relationship. She was still dealing with the loss of her husband.

Pulling a card from one of the other arrangements, Meagan smiled as she read it. "All our love, Mom and Dad." It was made up of peach-colored roses, and she set it in the middle of the table in the reception area.

Her heart did a somersault when she read the card for the next arrangement silently. *Best wishes. Welcome home. Nick.* She felt the color flood her cheeks and heard her heartbeat pounding in her ears as she looked around for a place to set Nick's beautiful bouquet. While Ronni was busy bringing in more of the arrangements, Meagan quickly took the one she held in her hands back to the desk in her office. She decided to figure out where to put it later on and hurried back to help Ronni with the rest of the flowers.

As they placed the floral arrangements around the shop, Meagan glanced at her watch several times. In less than half an hour they'd be opening the doors for business.

"I think we'll wait to uncover the windows until right before we open," Meagan said as the left Ronni to finish up with the flowers and went to the small kitchen in the back. She pulled out the large urn she'd rented and put the coffee on to perk. Laura and Sara, the two other full-time consultants she'd hired, would be bringing in the cookies she'd ordered from the bakery.

Meagan hoped she hadn't made a mistake by deciding to have refreshments. She'd hate to see any of her stock ruined by carelessness. Since she'd advertised free coffee and cookies, she'd just remain optimistic and take the loss if anything got ruined.

As the aroma of freshly brewed coffee filtered through the shop, Laura and Sara arrived with the cookies. Sara was a wonderful example of a Cool Summer, dressed in a powder blue suit that enhanced her translucent skin, ash blond hair, and soft gray eyes. Dark-eyed, raven-haired Laura wore a vibrant red to bring out her Cool Winter coloring.

Looking at the women who would help her run the shop, Meagan could see they were almost as excited as she was. She was sure she couldn't have picked three better examples of Summer, Autumn, and Winter coloring if she'd interviewed a hundred other women.

"Well, ladies, we have about twenty minutes before we open. We'd better hustle." She made a mental checklist of what needed to be done. A drawing was to be held every hour for a free consultation. From those, demonstrations would be given so that the customers could see what Meagan's Color Cottage was all about.

"Ronni, will you get out the entry forms and box for the drawings and get that set up? And, Sara, Laura, would you set up the refreshment table?"

The three women went about their work, and Meagan stepped through to one of the display windows to begin taking down the brown paper covering. As she removed the paper from the other window, she looked out to meet the smiles and waves of several people waiting for her to open the door. Smiling and waving back, Meagan felt a sense of belonging that she hadn't experienced in a long time.

She turned the OPEN side of the door sign around to face the street and opened the door just as Mayor Eddington and a reporter and photographer from the *Sun Herald* arrived. Quick introductions were made and congratulations given. A wide yellow ribbon was brought out and stretched across the opening. Customers started gathering around to watch while the photographer took pictures of Meagan with the mayor, of Meagan with her employees, and finally the ribbon-cutting ceremony.

Excited and happy, Meagan smiled at the crowd and waved when she spotted her mom and dad. There were tears in her mother's eyes and a camera in front of her dad's. She thought she saw him blink several times after he lowered the camera, but she knew she saw a great deal of love and pride shining from her parents' eyes.

She hugged them quickly then turned and began greeting her customers. The moment had come. Finally, Meagan's Color Cottage of Magnolia Bay was open for business.

❧

Nick faced Jeff across the wide expanse of his desk. Elbows

resting on the arms of his chair, his fingertips grazed his chin as he contemplated the man he'd called his friend for years. "Why didn't you tell me Meagan was moving back?"

Jeff looked into Nick's accusing gaze and shrugged. "I assumed you knew. Her name is all over the contracts I've been drawing up."

"Jeff, I was aware we were representing a new shop in town, but you know I don't feel the need, nor do I have the time, to check every contract you draw up. I had no idea Meagan *Evans* was the owner." He exhaled deeply and shook his head. "You should have told me."

"Nick, Meagan's name hasn't been mentioned between us for years." He sighed. "I didn't know whether you even thought about her anymore."

Nick got up and walked over to his office window. It was still hard to believe she was actually back here—only a few blocks away on Bay Drive. He turned back to Jeff.

"I seem to remember you telling me I'd live to regret breaking up with Meagan." The anger was gone, but Nick couldn't keep a note of sadness from creeping into his voice.

"And I remember you telling me to mind my own business and leave Meagan out of our conversations. I figured if you ever changed your mind, you'd be the one to bring the subject up."

"It looks like you were right all the way around." Nick watched Jeff's eyes widen at his admission. It wasn't easy for Nick to admit he was wrong about anything, and he very rarely did, except to himself and the Lord. He went over to the coffeemaker and poured two cups then handed Jeff one and sat back down at his desk. Nick leaned back in his chair and closed his eyes. "I don't think I ever got over her."

"I suspected that from your reaction the other night."

"Are you two dating?" Nick felt he had to ask. He'd been wondering about it ever since seeing them on Saturday night. Nick's irritation at his friend inched upward as Jeff chuckled.

"Meagan and I do see each other from time to time." Jeff grinned and then shook his head. "She's like a sister to me, Nick."

Nick didn't realize he'd been holding his breath until he released it. Suddenly, he felt the need to explain his past actions to Jeff. "Did I ever tell you why I stopped seeing Meagan?"

Jeff shook his head. "You didn't have to. I knew she scared you."

"What I felt for her certainly did. I don't think she ever realized it, though."

"No, you hid it pretty well." Jeff took a drink of his coffee before continuing. "You should have told her."

Nick surprised himself by saying, "I didn't have the guts." He rubbed his fingers over his forehead. "Besides, it wouldn't have changed anything. I was too young to handle the depth of my feelings for her, and much too young to realize how special they were."

Jeff nodded. "That's what I thought."

"I've never felt that way about anyone again." Nick got up again and began to pace back and forth in front of the window. While it felt good to tell someone how he felt, he knew he wouldn't go into all the reasons for their breakup with his friend. Meagan was the one he owed an explanation to, and she might never give him the chance to—not after all this time. He walked over and sat on the edge of his desk. Nick felt the same frustration he'd felt back then, only it was worse now. He knew what he'd given up.

"Looks like she still has a hold on you," Jeff said.

Nick met his friend's gaze. "More than I realized. I've got to find out if she feels anything but hate for me after all these years. And I'm going to need all the help I can get to do it."

four

Meagan leaned back in her wicker rocker, reflecting on the day. Shortly after she'd closed up and finished her daily call to her Dallas employees, Thad had called to find out how the day had gone and she'd thanked him for the huge arrangement of roses that had been delivered that afternoon. She'd told him the highlights of the opening but now, refreshed from a shower and relaxing on the balcony with a cup of tea, she was able to send a prayer heavenward, thanking the Lord for such a glorious opening for Meagan's Color Cottage.

The day had gone even better than she'd hoped. A whole month of appointments had been scheduled for color consultations, but most customers weren't waiting to buy. Meagan was amazed at the total sales for the day.

She and her employees had been so busy with potential customers, Meagan didn't know what she would have done without her family. Her mother had taken over serving refreshments, making everyone feel welcome and wanted—and a myriad of small things no one else had time to do. Even her dad and uncle had gotten into the act, making repeated trips to the bakery for more cookies. Claudia Melrose—Ronni's mother-in-law and one of Meagan's late grandmother's best friends—had pitched in and helped, too.

Meagan closed her eyes and smiled. How lucky she was to have such a supporting family. She'd worried about overtiring them until she finally recognized the excitement and pride in their eyes as they'd told her to leave them alone—they were having the time of their lives. It wasn't until closing time when her uncle Mark came in bearing hamburgers for everyone that she realized none of them had eaten anything but an occasional cookie all day.

It turned out to be a wonderful grand-opening party with her family and employees eating, laughing, and relating stories about the day. A contented sigh escaped her lips. There'd been so many people in and out, new customers and old friends. She was almost sure she'd caught a glimpse of Nick that afternoon, but when she looked again, no one was there. *Better watch that ego, Meagan,* she told herself. *Just because you want him to see how much you've accomplished without him, doesn't mean he wants to know. He lost interest in you long ago. Why would it matter now?*

Irritated by the tears that suddenly sprang to her eyes, Meagan assured herself that they were just the result of a long, exciting, and tiring day. Tucking thoughts of Nick into the back of her mind, she willed herself to think of Thad and his proposal; how she wished he'd been able to be here today to see the opening.

Finally, she made a mental list of all of her blessings and that effectively stopped the tears and brought a smile to her face. A special dream had come true today, and she would concentrate on it. Now was not the time to think about broken dreams of the past.

&

The next few days were so busy, Meagan was surprised—and more than a little irritated—by how often thoughts of Nick interrupted her work. For years, she'd been able to force thoughts of him to the back of her mind, but suddenly, she

was finding it almost impossible to *not* think of him. And it
wasn't Nick, but Thad she should be thinking of. She prayed
that the Lord would direct her thoughts to the man who'd
asked her to marry him.

The flowers from Nick certainly didn't help. Every
morning the florist met her at the shop just as she unlocked
the front door. A different, lavish, flower arrangement
would be presented to her, along with a card that read *Have
a good day. Nick.* Today's message had been different; it said,
I'll call tonight. Meagan wondered if he really would; he'd
never been very good about calling when he said he would
in the past. Then again, he'd been a high school senior at
the time, she a mere freshman, she reminded herself.

"Meagan," Ronni said, interrupting her thoughts as she
set a cup of coffee on her desk. "Your mom called while you
were making the deposit. She said she'd be in tomorrow
and that if we need her help before then, just to call."

"I think we may have to stay open until around nine a
night or two a week, Ronni. That means I need to hire and
train one or two part-time employees. Those first three days
we could have used six more people. I can't continue to put
Mom or Claudia to work every time they come in."

She took a sip of coffee and rubbed the back of her neck.
Business had slowed somewhat from the first day, but was
still brisk enough to keep Meagan there until closing every
evening. Or that's what she told herself. Living upstairs
did have its drawbacks—she didn't seem to know when
to call it a day. Even when she closed the doors at six, she
found things she needed to do. Of course, she loved it right
now, but she knew she wouldn't want to work at this pace
forever.

"We did file all the applications we took, didn't we?" At

Ronni's nod, she went to the file cabinet, found the folder she was looking for, and dropped it on her desk. "I'll go over these later. Do you think we should hire high school girls, or someone older?"

Before Ronni could give her an answer, they were interrupted by the arrival of Meagan's next appointment for a color consultation. She'd scheduled appointments for the rest of the afternoon, pleased that one of them was with Alice Benson. She hadn't talked to her friend since the night of the reunion except only briefly the day of the grand opening.

Now she smiled as she went to greet her present customer then led her to one of the mirrored cubicles. Meagan pulled different groups of fabric from underneath the counter and began by draping one of the large triangle-shaped swatches around the woman's neck. This was the part of her business she really loved. Helping women look their best by showing them how the right colors of clothing and cosmetics complemented their features was the most rewarding aspect of her business. The looks of surprise or delight on their faces at seeing how a different shade or a color they'd never thought of wearing enhanced their own coloring, never failed to please her.

When Alice breezed in an hour later, she was flushed and smiling.

"Marriage and children must agree with you, Alice," Meagan commented after seating her friend in one of the cubicles. "I've never seen anyone look so content and happy."

Alice laughed. "Oh, I have my bad days. Days when the twins are into everything, the house is an absolute mess, and Mike calls to say his hostess didn't show up and asks if

I can come to the restaurant and help out!"

"Sounds like you stay busy from morning until night."

Alice grinned at Meagan through the mirror. "I wouldn't change a thing, though."

Meagan smiled back at her. "No. I didn't think so." She began draping the color swatches around Alice's neck. It didn't take long for Alice to agree that her coloring truly was a Cool Summer.

"You've instinctively chosen the right colors for yourself. You'd be surprised how many women are swayed by the color that is *in* at the moment or are just in love with a color that is totally wrong for them."

Alice nodded. "I know what you mean. I do hope Debbie comes in. She is so pretty, but that color she had on the other night was terrible on her. Since you're an expert on the subject, maybe she'll listen to you."

Mention of the night they all got together brought thoughts of Nick to the fore, and almost as if she could read Meagan's mind, Alice asked, "Was it hard to see Nick again?"

"It was. . .uncomfortable," Meagan admitted hesitantly.

"It must have been hard for him, too. He left right after you and Jeff did. I think he was as shocked to see you as you were to see him. He's not the same Nick we went to school with."

Meagan hadn't given much thought to how seeing her might have affected Nick. She'd been too busy trying not to think about her reaction to seeing him. Now all she could find to say was, "Oh?"

Her friend waved her hand in the air as she answered Meagan's unspoken question as to how she knew so much about Nick. "He and Mike were roommates in college.

They've remained good friends. He really has changed, Meagan. Like all of us, he had to grow up," Alice added softly.

Meagan couldn't help commenting. "He didn't have a very easy time of it, I guess."

Alice shook her head. "No, he didn't. But once he accepted that he had responsibilities, he did a terrific job of taking them on. You know he took over his grandfather's firm and proved to everyone that he was more than competent. He's made a name for himself all along the Gulf Coast, already." She paused a moment, and her gaze met Meagan's in the mirror. "He became a Christian, too."

For so long, she'd prayed that Nick would come to the Lord. Now Meagan's heart expanded with such intense joy she couldn't speak for a moment. All she could do was smile at Alice. And she wanted to know more, but she suddenly felt guilty for discussing Nick when she was practically engaged to another man. Meagan changed the subject abruptly. "Let me show you what wonderful things I have in your color season."

If Alice suspected she'd hit a raw nerve by bringing up Nick, she didn't show it, and the conversation turned to fashion, hairstyles, and accessories. Alice bought several items, and they had a cup of coffee together before she left. Meagan was relieved that the subject of Nick didn't come up again.

The rest of the afternoon and evening seemed to fly by, yet Meagan felt she'd accomplished a lot as she closed up. She'd found time to go over the job applications and found a couple that she felt might work out. Luckily they'd been interested in part-time work. She'd contacted them and had set interviews for both of them for the next day. Feeling satisfied with her day's work, she turned out the lights, locked up, and headed upstairs to her apartment.

❧

Nick resisted the urge to slam the phone receiver down. He was aware he was overreacting, but he'd been trying to call Meagan at the number Jeff had given him for several hours. It was her home phone—he didn't want to bother her at work—but it was past closing time, and he was beginning to wonder if she was trying to avoid him. He told himself that was a defeatist attitude. She probably just worked late. Avoidance had always been *his* style in years past, not Meagan's.

Finding it almost impossible to concentrate on the work he'd brought home, Nick pushed back his chair and picked up his still full, but cold, coffee cup. He wondered at the silence as he walked through the house to the kitchen.

There, sitting at the kitchen table, was the reason for all the quiet. His grandmother was engrossed in reading the evening newspaper and Tori was actually studying. At least that's what it looked like she was doing, which Nick found hard to believe. He sauntered over and put his hand on his little sister's forehead before she and their grandmother realized he was in the room. "Tori, honey, are you all right?"

Tori's look was puzzled and his grandmother's one of concern. "What's wrong, Nick? Does she have a fever?"

Nick winked at his grandmother. "No. But I thought she must be sick or something, giving that much attention to her homework."

"Oh, Nicky!" Tori flung off his hand.

"Actually, I think it's *or someone,*" Hattie Chambers said. "There's a cute new boy at school. A very smart one, it seems."

Nick watched his little sister blush as he took a seat at the table. Was she really at that age already?

His grandmother slid the paper she'd been reading over to him before getting up to bring a plate of still warm cookies to the table and pour him a fresh cup of coffee. She sat back down at the table and pointed at the picture he was studying. "Is that the Meagan you said you knew? She looks familiar, somehow."

"She should. I had her picture up in my room for a long time." The photograph in the paper was one taken the day Meagan's shop opened. He read the article describing the shop and a brief history of what Meagan had been doing since she'd graduated. It stressed the fact that she'd answered her grandmother's call to try to help Magnolia Bay come back to life. His gaze strayed back to the picture. She was striking, even in newspaper print. There was something in her eyes and her smile that seemed to reach out from within. Nick felt a tug at his heart as he tore his gaze away from the picture.

He looked up to find his grandmother watching him closely. Could she see the pain he felt? He hoped not. Nick quickly averted his eyes and asked, "You wouldn't know what happened to all the high school things I had in my room in the other house, would you, Gran?"

His grandmother's eyes took on a knowing look. "I'm sure it's all up in the attic somewhere. I didn't throw anything out. Would you like me to look for something for you?"

Trying not to rouse her curiosity, Nick shook his head. "No. Don't worry about it. I'll look one of these days."

Feeling more restless than before, he glanced at his watch. Maybe Meagan would be home by now. He'd told her he would call tonight, and he intended to keep calling until she answered. Swallowing the last of his coffee, he stood up and took the cup to the sink.

Tori reached for the paper, and now she looked at Nick with new respect. "You really knew Meagan Evans that well? You had her picture in your room?"

Nick grinned and nodded.

"Nicky, will you please take me to meet her sometime?"

"Oh, *now* you finally believe me, do you?" He couldn't help grinning at the excitement in her eyes.

"Please, Nick," she implored.

"We'll see." Nick ruffled her hair and dropped a kiss on her head. If things worked out only half as well as he hoped, Tori would definitely get to meet Meagan.

He settled back in his study and tried her number once more. The need to hear her voice grew with each ring. Would she even agree to see him? And would she believe him after all these years? He certainly couldn't blame her if she didn't. He hadn't always been honest with her in the past, but that was before the boy had turned into the man—and long before the man had become a Christian. That alone could be the biggest problem. She'd only known the boy, and because of that, she might never want to know the man. . . .

five

Meagan hurriedly unlocked the door to her apartment, hoping to reach the phone before it stopped ringing. Her heart did a funny little double beat as she looked at the last bunch of roses she'd brought upstairs and picked up the receiver. It did a triple beat when she recognized Nick's voice on the other end.

"Meagan, I hope I'm not disturbing you."

Meagan was having trouble understanding the rush of pleasure she felt at the sound of his voice and the surprise that he'd kept his word and did call. "No, you aren't. In fact, I just walked in the door."

She set the arrangement on the table beside her chair and added, "Oh, thank you for the flowers, Nick. They are lovely."

"You're welcome." Nick paused for a moment. "Opening a new business must be totally exhausting."

Meagan slipped off her shoes and eased her tired body into her recliner. "It is, but I'm enjoying every ache and pain."

Nick chuckled. "That bad, huh? You're putting in a lot of long hours, aren't you?"

"I have been. Living up over the shop, I find it a little hard to call it a day and come upstairs. Actually, I don't think I'd have left any earlier this week even if I'd had twice the help." Meagan wondered why it felt so right to be casually talking to Nick after all these years until she remembered that they'd always been able to talk to each other about all kinds of things—until they'd starting going together.

"Sounds as if business continues to be good," Nick said, his voice warm and husky.

How could she possibly resist talking about the subject closest to her heart at the moment? "It is, Nick. In fact, I hired a part-time employee today so we can start staying open late a couple of nights a week. I start training her tomorrow."

"That's wonderful, Meagan. I'm really happy that things are gong so well. I saw the write-up in the paper about you. Do you remember my little sister, Tori? She'd sure love to meet you. She was quite impressed, judging from her reaction to finding out I know you."

"Oh, how sweet. Of course I remember Tori. Jeff said she was almost sixteen?" Meagan could only remember her as a sweet and cuddly toddler.

"That's right. And I don't think she's ever really going to believe I do know you unless I introduce her to you."

"I'd love to see her again. It's hard to imagine the little one I remember as a teenager."

Nick chuckled. "What's hard is realizing *I'm* raising a teenager."

"I think the trick to that is in remembering what it was like to be a teenager." Meagan could have bit her tongue for letting go with that piece of advice. She felt even worse when she heard the regret in Nick's voice.

"Oh, I remember. I just hope she has more sense than I did."

"Nick, I. . ." Meagan didn't know what else to say.

The tension across the line was almost tangible until

Nick changed the subject. "Now that you are going to have extra help, does that mean you might have some free time?"

"I hope so," Meagan said before she realized what he might be leading up to. Talking on the phone was one thing. Talking in person was quite another. She just wasn't ready to tackle that one. "Probably not for a while, though. There's the training and making sure the new girls can handle things by themselves, if they have to."

"Yes, that will probably take awhile," Nick agreed. "I know you've got a busy day ahead of you tomorrow. I won't keep you. Try to pace yourself and don't work too hard. I'll bring Tori by one of these days, if you are sure it's all right."

"Thanks, Nick. And of course it's all right. Bring Tori by anytime." Surely, he wouldn't bring up the past with his sister around.

"She'll be thrilled. Thank you, Meagan. Good night," Nick said softly.

Meagan sat staring at the phone after she hung up. She hated the confusion she was feeling. Even though she didn't want to talk about the past with Nick, it had felt good to talk about the present. He'd sounded as though he really was interested in her business and concerned that she might be working too hard.

They'd been such good friends before they started seeing each other. She wished they'd never dated because she missed the special friendship they'd once shared.

Meagan sighed as she pushed herself out of her chair, feeling guilty that Nick was on her mind so often when it was Thad she should be thinking about. Instead, she hadn't given him a thought until just now.

She sat back down and dialed Thad's number. It rang several times before his answering machine came on. He must be out to dinner or something. She left a quick message letting him know that she was thinking about him, but when she replaced the receiver, she wasn't sure if she was let down or relieved that he wasn't home.

❧

The next two days were hectic. Trying to take care of the consultations she had set up and training a new employee at the same time was enough to make Meagan realize she couldn't keep working at her present pace.

Ronni finally talked her into a coffee break after she let the new employee go home for the day. Meagan closed her eyes while she inhaled the rich aroma of freshly brewed coffee. "Mmm, you make a mean cup of coffee, Ronni."

"It's the only thing I could think of that would get you to sit down for a few minutes. Meagan, you really need to slow down. I know you're excited and that you've worked a long time to see this dream come true. It's not going to disappear tomorrow. You have hired very competent employees, if I do say so myself." She grinned at Meagan. "And you are going to have to pace yourself if you want to make it to the Christmas season."

Meagan opened her mouth to speak, but Ronni rushed on before she had a chance to get a word out.

"Laura and Sara can take care of things this evening." As Meagan again began to speak, Ronni held up a hand. "I know it's the first night we are staying open until nine, but you need to show them you trust them. Why don't you come have dinner with me and Claudia?" she asked as she perched on the edge of Meagan's desk.

Meagan sighed. She *was* tired. And she'd be right upstairs if Laura or Sara needed her. "You're right. I do have wonderful employees, and it's time I entrusted them with taking care of things when I'm not here. Thank you for the invite, but I believe I'm more tired than I am hungry. I think I'll just take a long shower and go to bed early." She stood up and gave Ronni a quick hug. "Thanks for the lecture."

She looked at her watch and realized it was already six o'clock. Stifling a yawn, she said, "I'm going to show you I do trust my employees. I'm going upstairs right now." Grinning at Ronni to show her there were no hard feelings, Meagan walked to the front of the shop and told Laura and Sara they were in charge for the evening, waved, and headed up the stairs to her apartment.

Just climbing them made her realize how exhausted she really was. The September evenings were still warm, but the breeze off the water seemed to cool things down so that she could enjoy sitting outdoors. She poured a glass of iced tea and sat out on the balcony for a bit, letting the sound of the waves relax her. She barely had the energy to make herself get up to take a shower, and even that didn't revive her. After dressing in a soft, lemon yellow jogging suit, she made herself a cup of instant cappuccino and took it to her favorite recliner. Raising the footrest, she picked up the remote control and tuned in a movie she'd been hoping to catch. Ten minutes into it, she could no longer keep her eyes open.

A persistent rapping on the door brought her out of a deep sleep. Groggily, Meagan opened her eyes and realized someone was knocking on her outside door. Running her fingers through her hair and yawning, she made herself sit up. The rapping continued as she rubbed her eyes and went to open the door. The delicious smell wafting around her made her mouth water. Pizza? Had she ordered one and forgotten about it?

Meagan shook her head in an effort to clear it of sleep. She raised her gaze to whom she thought must be the delivery boy—and looked straight into the warm brown eyes of Nick Chambers.

❧

Nick watched Meagan run her fingers through her tousled hair. It was obvious he'd awakened her. She seemed to be trying to pull her thoughts together.

"Nick. I, ahh. . . What are you doing here?"

The tenderness he'd always felt for Meagan grew as he took in her confused state and disheveled appearance. "I ran into Ronni—is that her name?" At Meagan's nod, he continued, "Anyway, she said you'd called it a day and that you were pretty tired."

Meagan nodded.

Nick lifted the pizza box into the air and grinned at her. "Well, I took the chance that while you might be tired, you haven't changed so much that you could turn down a pizza."

The aroma drifting from the box couldn't be ignored. He heard Meagan's stomach rumble, and she opened the door wider. "I was tired, but my catnap helped. And, you are right, I never could turn down pizza."

Nick hesitated briefly. "If you don't want company, I can just leave the pizza."

"And leave me feeling guilty for depriving you of *your* favorite food? No way." Meagan chuckled and headed for the kitchen. "Why don't you take it out onto the balcony. We can eat out there. Do you want iced tea, or a soft drink?"

"Tea, please."

He placed the pizza box on the table between the wicker rockers, then stood looking out at the bay that led into the

Gulf of Mexico. Soon she joined him, carrying drinks, paper plates, and napkins.

"You have a nice place. The view is wonderful from here."

"Thank you. I love it." She motioned for him to sit down. "Come on. Let's eat."

Nick sank down onto the rocker. "May I say a prayer first?"

Meagan's face beamed. "Yes, please do."

After offering thanks, Nick opened the box. "Ladies first," he said as he slid a large piece of pizza onto a plate and handed it to her.

Meagan inhaled the mouthwatering aroma from the sausage, mushroom, and pepperoni pizza as she took the plate. It was several moments before she said anything but, "Mmm," and Nick watched her in delight. When she'd finished one piece, she looked up at Nick and found him grinning at her. "What?"

"It's just nice to know some things never change," he said, then took his first bite.

Meagan smiled and helped herself to another piece. "It's nice that you remembered my favorite kind of pizza."

They drifted into comfortable conversation as they took turns eating and talking. Nick asked about her part-time help, the business, and her parents.

"What made you decide to open a business here?"

"I'd always planned to, but it was Grammy Simmons who convinced me to do it now. She wanted Magnolia Bay to come back to life, and she and several others had formed a committee to try to draw businesses into the town. I only wish she'd lived long enough to see if their plans work."

"I'm sorry about the loss of your grandmother, Meagan."

"Thank you. And I'm so sorry about your losses, too." She

asked Nick about his work, his grandmother, and his sister.

"Bring Tori in anytime, Nick. I'll give her a free color consultation."

"What's that?"

Meagan laughed. "Most men ask that same question. It's where we'll find out what colors look the very best on her to bring out her own natural beauty."

"She'd love that," Nick said. "And maybe it will give her a little more confidence in herself."

"That's what my business is all about." Meagan leaned back from the pizza box and moaned. "As usual, when it comes to pizza, I ate too much. Thank you for bringing it by, Nick."

He shook his head. "No thanks needed. I'm just glad you let me join you."

Meagan started gathering up their mess.

"Let me help," Nick said.

"No, that's fine. I'll be right back," Meagan said and took the remnants of their meal to the kitchen.

❧

Nick was leaning against the railing when she rejoined him. He turned and smiled at her. "It's really nice out here."

Meagan nodded. "It is. I love—"

"The surf," he finished for her as he turned around. "You know, your love of pizza and gulf beaches isn't all I remember about you, Meagan."

She avoided his gaze and sat down in the rocker she'd vacated earlier. Nick sat back down and stared out at the bay, rubbing his palms over his thighs before clasping them in front of his knees. He turned and his gaze met hers.

"I know that talking about the past is probably the last thing you want to do. I wish there was no need for it myself.

But, Meagan, there was just too much left unsaid."

"Nick—"

He reached across the table to gently touch her lips. An electric current shot through her at his touch, and her surprise kept her silent as he dropped his hand.

"Meagan, I've wanted a chance to say this for years. Please let me get it out." He stared into the distance for a moment before continuing. "I treated you badly all those years ago, and I know it. The only excuse I can give you is that I was an immature, self-centered jerk. And I know that's not good enough. I'm sorry—"

"Nick, there's no need—"

"Yes, there is a need, Meagan," Nick interrupted. He paused and looked her in the eyes. "And, as much as I hate to admit it, I'm still being selfish. I want your forgiveness, Meagan. Do you think you can ever give it to me?"

The bleak look in his eyes convinced Meagan he was sincere. He hadn't really answered any of the questions she'd asked herself over the years, but he'd said he was sorry and asked her to forgive him. That much she could do.

His gaze never wavered from hers. He could never have met her eyes if he'd been lying. When she smiled at him, he noticeably relaxed. "Nick, I forgave you long ago. Even before I got over the hurt of knowing you didn't care about me anymore."

Nick dropped his head into his hands and groaned. "Meagan, I never meant to hurt you. And our breakup was never because I *didn't* care about you."

Meagan stared out to sea. "Then why?"

Nick shook his head. "It *never* occurred to me that you would think that. Our breakup was because I cared so much."

She was more confused than ever. "Nick, that doesn't make sense."

He got up and leaned against the railing, facing her. "Meagan, what I felt for you scared me. All I thought of was you. I was insanely jealous of anyone you talked to."

"But you didn't want to spend all your time with me," Meagan gently reminded him.

Nick ran his fingers through his hair. "Meagan, I didn't know what I was doing. I know I smothered you, even ran off most of your friends. I felt as if I was drowning. And I was way too young to handle what I was feeling. I was thinking marriage. We were so young. . ." He broke off on the last word and turned to look out over the gently breaking waves.

Meagan joined him at the balcony's railing. She knew this wasn't easy for him. "Nick, it's all right. You don't have to go on."

"No." Nick took her hand in his and gripped it firmly. "You know how hard it was for me to accept my mother's death."

Meagan fought the tears that formed and nodded.

"What I never told you was that we'd had an argument the day before she had the heart attack, and I blamed myself when she died. I know it makes no sense, but I felt as though she'd left me—even though I knew better. Meagan, I was scared to death that you would find out what an awful person I was and I would lose you, too. I knew I was too demanding of you, that I treated you badly." He took a deep breath and reached over to cup Meagan's face in the palm of his hand. "You were the best thing that happened to me after my mom died. But I couldn't face your feelings turning to hate, as I was sure they eventually would—and probably did. So I destroyed everything while I thought I was in control and could still handle it." Nick dropped his hand from her face.

In the silence that followed, Meagan realized she didn't know what to say. Her heart broke at his words, and she tried to swallow around the huge lump in her throat. She wanted to believe him now, yet there was a tiny doubt in the back of her mind; he'd lied to her so many times in the past.

"Meagan, I know I hurt you. If it's any consolation, I think I hurt myself most of all. I damaged a caring relationship and one of the best friendships I'd ever had— all in one fell swoop."

Meagan's eyes were full of unshed tears for herself, for Nick, and for the past. "You know, I used to wish we'd just remained best friends."

Nick nodded and cleared his throat. "Do you think it'd be possible to salvage that friendship?"

"I'm not sure," Meagan answered honestly. "We really don't even know each other anymore."

Silence hung heavy in the air. The clock inside struck midnight, and Nick stretched. "I'd better go." He looked down into her eyes. "Would you be willing to try to be friends again?"

Meagan's heart lurched at his pleading look. She couldn't help wondering if she was making a mistake as she answered. "I guess we could try."

Nick squeezed her hand and led her back inside and to the door. He turned and brushed his lips lightly across her forehead. "Thank you, Meagan."

She caught her breath and could only nod as he opened the door.

"Good night." Nick took the stairs two at a time down to the parking lot.

Meagan stood there a moment before locking the door and turning to lean against it. Had Nick been telling her the truth? Would it be possible for them to be friends again?

She shook her head and began to straighten the apartment, automatically plumping up pillows, loading the dishwasher, and getting the coffeepot ready for the next morning, her thoughts going over and over everything Nick told her. And now he wanted to be friends again. Meagan had agreed to try, but did she really want to? Nick had been out of her life for a long time. Wouldn't it be better to keep him out?

She turned out the lights and went to her room to get ready for bed. It was only after she'd removed all her makeup that she recognized the flushed face and bright eyes of her youth. Yet, she wasn't a teenager anymore. She was an adult. And she wasn't about to let the sudden memory of his soft lips brushing her brow, or his warm hand holding her own, fluster her. She snapped out the light, went to bed, and said her prayers, asking the Lord to help her to quit thinking of what could have been and think about Thad and her future with him, instead.

six

Nick drove across town, feeling better than he had in years. He'd finally been able to apologize to Meagan. He'd been surprised that the conversation they'd shared over the pizza had been so easy and comfortable. He hadn't expected to feel at ease around her, yet he had. It kind of felt like old times—almost, but not quite.

Nick knew Meagan was leery of him—that she wasn't sure she could trust what he was saying. He'd seen it in her eyes, while he was trying to explain himself to her, when he'd held her hand, and kissed her at the door. In spite of her doubts, she'd agreed they could try to be friends again. He sent up a silent prayer thanking the Lord for the way everything turned out tonight.

He pulled into his drive, grinning to himself. Well, he'd always liked a challenge, hadn't he? What bigger challenge could he have than trying to regain Meagan's trust? He was determined to do just that—with the help of the Lord.

❧

Nick's actions the next week went a long way in convincing Meagan that he meant it when he said he'd like to be friends again. But was that what she wanted? Why did her pulse race each time the florist brought flowers from him or when she answered the phone at night and found it was Nick on the other end of the line instead of Thad? Why did her heart jump at the sound of Nick's voice but not Thad's?

Thad continued to call, but it was usually as soon as she

closed up the shop, while Nick had taken to calling her later in the evening. In spite of feeling disloyal to Thad, Meagan found herself looking forward to Nick's calls. She enjoyed discussing her day with him. He seemed genuinely interested in her work, and in turn, she liked hearing about his law firm, his work, and his family. His stories about Tori especially touched her.

"Anyway, Grams says Tori wants this Rod guy to ask her to homecoming, but she's afraid to even talk to him," Nick told her one night. He chuckled and then became serious. "She's just so unsure of herself, Meagan. I wish I knew how to help her. You had so much confidence at her age; what do you suggest?"

"Oh, Nick, no, I didn't. I was just as unsure of things as Tori is now," she admitted. "I probably just hid it better. But maybe I can help with this. I thought you were going to bring her in to meet me."

"I'm going to. In fact, she asks me about it every day. I know how busy you've been, and I don't want it to be a bad time for you."

"How about bringing her in tomorrow afternoon? I have plenty of help, and I should be able to give her a quick consultation and tour of the shop, if she'd like." Meagan found herself looking forward to seeing Tori.

"Meagan, she'd love it! I've got an appointment that might run late, though." Nick paused. "Would it be all right if my grandmother brings her in? I could pick her up right after my meeting."

"Of course," Meagan agreed. After all, Nick had a business to run, too.

It was about four the next afternoon when she looked up to see an older woman and a teenager standing hesitantly in the reception area. Even if she hadn't recognized Nick's grandmother, Meagan certainly would have known his sister. Her hair and eyes were darker than Nick's, but the full cut of her lips and the expressive eyebrows were just like his. Even her shy smile reminded Meagan of Nick's.

She held out her hand to the older woman. "Mrs. Chambers, it's so nice to see you again. It's been a long time, but you haven't changed a bit."

Hattie Chambers smiled. "That's sweet of you, Meagan. Even an old woman likes to hear those words." She laughed and patted Meagan's hand. "*Especially* an old woman."

Meagan impulsively leaned forward to kiss the older woman's cheek before turning to the young girl. "And you must be Tori."

Nick's little sister blushed, smiled, and nodded.

"Well, you certainly have changed." Meagan bent over and placed her hand about three feet off the floor. "You were about this tall last time I saw you."

"Really?" Tori asked.

"Really," Meagan confirmed. She poured Nick's grandmother a cup of coffee and got a soft drink for Tori. "I thought I'd show you around the shop and then give Tori a color consultation, if that's all right with you, Tori." So as not to hurt the young girl's feelings, she added quickly, "Not that you don't know what colors are best for you—just to show you what I do."

"I *don't* know what colors to pick, do I, Grams? I'd love a consultation," Tori said excitedly.

"Well, what are we waiting for?" Meagan led the way into the interior of the shop. She enjoyed giving the two of them a tour. Mrs. Chambers and Tori seemed really interested in everything she showed them as she explained what Meagan's Color Cottage was all about.

"I believe that God has given every woman a beauty uniquely her own. My job is helping my clients find the outside beauty that reflects that uniqueness inside. Helping a woman discover the colors that enhance what the Lord has already provided her with is truly rewarding."

Meagan was a little disappointed when Nick's grandmother pulled her aside, while Tori was busy looking through a rack of teen fashions, to tell her she was leaving.

"I told Nick I'd be glad to stay and bring her home, but he insisted he'd pick her up." Mrs. Chambers glanced over at her granddaughter before whispering, "I think she might be more comfortable if I do leave before this makeover. You know how teenagers are."

Meagan smiled at the older woman's insight. "You might be right. Some clients do become self-conscious if someone else is around."

"Besides, she really does need to do a few things on her own, without Nick or me standing right over her shoulder." Nick's grandmother smiled at Meagan. "I feel like I'm leaving her in good hands."

"Thank you." Meagan felt as though she'd been paid a great compliment.

Indeed, Tori did seem to relax somewhat after her grandmother left. Meagan motioned for her to sit in one of the swivel chairs and turned it toward the mirror. "Ready?"

Excitement flashed in the young girl's eyes as she nodded at Meagan.

Meagan couldn't remember when she'd so much fun working. Tori proved to be an enthusiastic pupil. After cleansing off the makeup she had worn in and leaving off foundation so they could see Tori's natural skin tone, Meagan draped several different colored triangles of cloth around her neck to show her which ones enhanced her skin tone. The clear, primary colors were the ones that seemed to make Tori glow. "You are what we call a Cool Winter."

"I've never worn such vivid colors before," Tori said, looking in the mirror at her reflection with a Chinese blue swatch at her neck. "I've always worn lighter colors."

Meagan nodded and brought out another group of swatches. These were icy tones, almost white but with a drop of color to them. She held several around Tori's neck and watched her smile as she saw her coloring come alive. "These would be your version of pastels."

Tori looked up at Meagan and smiled. "Oh, I really like these colors, and the deeper ones, too. I just never thought they would look good on me."

"I've always loved this color." Tori reached over and picked up a deep hot pink swatch then draped it around her neck. "It does look nice on me, doesn't it?"

Meagan hugged her shoulders. "Honey, it looks beautiful on you."

When Tori hugged her back, Meagan had to blink quickly to keep the tears from forming. Whether it was because the young girl had never really known her own mother, the fact that she was Nick's little sister, or that she remembered how attached she'd been to Tori as a young child, Meagan didn't know. All she did know was that her heart went out to the teenager.

"Do you think you could help me with the rest of my makeup, Miss Meagan? And maybe give me some ideas about my hair."

The next hour flew by as Meagan taught Tori how to apply makeup as sparingly as possible to make the most of her natural beauty. She let Tori try on several different lip and cheek colors. It was obvious to them both that the medium pink lip gloss and the plum blush brought out Tori's coloring perfectly.

Meagan then taught her how to French braid her hair. First she turned Tori so that she could see the back of her head in the mirror and watch what Meagan was doing. Then all Meagan's work was torn down, and she led Tori's hands through the process. It was when Tori finally tried it herself that Nick's name came up.

"You know, after I read the article about you and Nicky told me he knew you, I thought he was teasing me," Tori said, as her fingers worked to learn what Meagan had shown her. "But he really was telling me the truth."

Meagan laughed. "Yes, he was. We were good friends in school." She didn't need to tell Tori that her brother had broken her heart all those years ago. It certainly would serve no purpose now.

Tori continued weaving her hair. "How old were you when you knew each other?"

Meagan watched Tori deftly weave the three sections of hair as if she'd been doing it for years. "We were in high school."

Tori grinned, impishly. "Tell me. I know he's handsome now, but was my brother a cutie or a geek back then?"

Meagan laughed and shook her head. "I'm not sure Nick would want me to tell that," she teased.

"Oh no! That must mean he was *not* a cutie," Tori moaned. "My brother, the geek!"

Meagan patted her shoulder. "No, honey. Actually, he was considered quite a catch back then." *And still would be,* she added to herself.

Tori smiled. "He's a pretty good big brother," she said. "What do you think he'll say about the new me?"

"What could he possibly say, except that you look beautiful?" Meagan showed Tori how to coil the bottom of her braid up and tuck it in for a different look. She anchored it with pins and turned Tori's chair so she could see her reflection from all sides. The young teen's inner sweetness shone through, giving a glimpse of the lovely person God made her to be.

"Oh, Miss Meagan, I do look nice." Tori smiled, delightedly. She got up from the chair and hugged Meagan again. Her eyes were misty when she pulled back. "I didn't think I could ever look like this. I don't know how to thank you!"

"That's all the thanks I need, Tori." Meagan didn't know when she'd felt so good about helping someone find her own beauty. She bent over and opened a drawer then pulled out a smaller collection of the fabric swatches she'd used on Tori. "Here, these are your colors. You can use them as a guide when you are shopping for new clothes."

"Thank you! I think I'll look around while I'm waiting on Nick, if that's all right. Maybe I can talk him into buying a few things."

Meagan laughed. "Sounds good to me. If you need any help, just let me know."

"I will."

She smiled as Tori headed for the clothes in her color section. Tori smiled and held her head a little higher when Ronni and several customers commented on how nice she looked, filling Meagan with a warmth she knew was more than mere pride in a job well done. She was as proud of the girl as she would have been if Tori were *her* little sister.

Meagan couldn't wait for Nick to see her.

It was after six when he stepped into the shop. Meagan was standing outside one of the dressing rooms and waved him over when she saw him looking around.

She tried to hide a smile as she watched several women in the shop take a second look at Nick. Not too many men came in by themselves, and none as striking as Nick. *Oh yes, he would be considered a catch. More so than ever,* she thought as he made his way across the store. The width of his shoulders in his sports coat seemed magnified as he walked past the racks of feminine garments, and as he stepped into the section where Meagan was, she wondered what it would be like to have him to lean on, to help shoulder her fears and worries.

Nick smiled at her and glanced at his watch. "I'm sorry I'm so late getting here. My meeting ran longer than I expected."

Meagan smiled back. "Don't worry about it. It's been fun," she said, watching him look around the store.

He turned back to her. "Did Tori go home with Grams?"

"I'm afraid you aren't going to be so lucky." Meagan pointed to the dressing room and chuckled at Nick's puzzled look. "Tori's found a few things she likes."

Nick grinned and raised an eyebrow. "Oh, she has, has she? I knew I should have canceled that meeting."

The door to the dressing room flew open, and Tori burst out, her eyes glowing. "Nicky, I'm glad you're here! What do you. . ." She stopped midsentence, looking closely at her brother, and her hand flew to her hair. "What's wrong? Don't you like it?"

Meagan chewed her bottom lip, wondering about Nick's dazed look, hoping he wouldn't hurt Tori's feelings.

Nick reached out and captured Tori's small hand in his larger one. He shook his head as if to clear it then smiled as he turned Tori first one way and then another. "Nothing's wrong, sweetie. I really like it. It's just that I never realized how much you look like Mom."

Tori laughed a bit self-consciously, but the light was back in her eyes. She shook her head. "No, I don't. Mom was beautiful."

Nick's fingers gently raised her chin and looked into her eyes. "That's right. And so are you."

Meagan saw tears well up in Tori's eyes and had to blink several times to stop her own from forming.

Nick cleared his throat as Tori threw her arms around him.

"Thank you, Nicky." She kissed his cheek before pulling back and twirling in front of him. "What do you think of this outfit?"

Meagan left them to make their own choices, her footsteps silent on the thick carpet. Ronni was waiting for her.

"That's Nick Chambers," Ronni stated, rather than asked. At Meagan's nod, she added, "He's a fine-looking man."

"He is that." Meagan glanced back at Nick and grinned, remembering her earlier conversation with his sister. "Tori asked me if he'd been a cutie or a geek as a boy."

"Only the young would ask. That man couldn't have been a geek if he'd tried." Ronni laughed and shook her head. "Are you seeing him again?"

The question brought Meagan's head around with a jerk, and she felt the color flood her face, knowing she'd been caught watching Nick. "No. No!" *I'm practically engaged to Thad. . .and I haven't told my friends. I—why not? I. . . .*

Ronni was watching her closely.

"We're just friends." Meagan chewed her bottom lip again.

"Or not even that, really. I mean, we agreed to *try* to become friends again." And that's all they could be.

"Friends, huh?" Ronni asked skeptically as Nick and Tori approached the counter. Tori was grinning, and Nick's gaze was focused on Meagan.

Meagan felt totally flustered as they approached; her heart felt heavy that she hadn't told anyone except her mother about Thad asking her to marry him. But now wasn't the time. She tried to hide her irritation with herself by concentrating on Tori and the small pile of clothes she deposited on the counter. She smiled at the teenager. "You talked him into more than I thought you would."

"Not nearly as much as she wanted." Nick leaned against the counter, the scent of his aftershave making it difficult for Meagan to concentrate.

"I told her she'd have to wait until Christmas for anything else. Since that's only a few months away, I probably should have made her wait for all of it."

"Nicky, what good would it do to know my colors and not have any of them?" Tori asked.

Nick grinned and drew his sister close for a quick hug. "That's the argument you used, and I have to admit it sounded logical at the time, but it is hard to believe that you don't have *anything* in *your* colors in that big walk-in closet of yours."

"Well, maybe there's a few things," Tori admitted as Meagan rang up the total.

"*Now* the truth comes out," Nick said as he handed Meagan a check card. "When it's too late to do anything about it," he teased.

The transaction finished, Meagan carefully bagged up Tori's purchases, enjoying the brother-sister banter. She reached under the counter and added a small package she'd wrapped earlier.

"This is for you, Tori." She winked at the young woman. "I thought it might be hard to ask him for lip gloss and mascara on top of all of this."

"Oh, Miss Meagan! That's so sweet of you, but you've done so much for me already. I—"

Meagan came around the counter and pushed the package into Tori's hands. "I had a great time this afternoon, and I want you to have this. There's only one thing I'd like for you to do for me."

"You name it, Miss—"

Meagan laughingly interrupted. "That's it. I really appreciate you showing me respect in that Southern way we have, but I'd really like you to just call me Meagan." She smiled at Tori. "I'm too young and you're too old for me to feel comfortable with you calling me *Miss*. Besides, I feel like we've become friends this afternoon, and friends don't call each other *Miss*. Okay?"

"Thank you, Mi—Meagan." Tori's smile was wide. "I'd love for us to be friends."

"Good." Meagan smiled.

Tori turned back to Nick. "Are you going to ask her now?"

"Miss Meagan." Nick grinned mischievously and bowed low before returning to full height and looking Meagan in the eye. He continued in a deeply exaggerated Southern drawl that set Meagan's pulse racing. "We feel we might have kept you from your dinner hour by my tardiness in picking up my sister. We would like to make that up to you by treating you to some of that wonderful, greasy, fast food they serve at the hamburger stand across the street, if that is acceptable to you."

Meagan couldn't help laughing. "Oh, I don't know—"

"It's Tori's favorite cuisine," Nick added.

Tori punched his arm, but she was laughing, too, as she turned to Meagan. "Please come with us."

"Well. . ." Meagan glanced at her watch and looked up to see Ronni standing behind Nick, vigorously nodding her head. Well, why not? What could be safer than having dinner at a busy fast-food place on the beach with Nick *and* his sister? Besides, she'd agreed to try to be friends again, hadn't she? "I'll be back in a little while, Ronni, okay?"

"Take your time. I can handle things here." Ronni grinned at her, and Meagan knew she'd have a ton of questions thrown at her when she got back. But Tori was looking at her expectantly, and Meagan didn't want to disappoint her.

"All right," she said, looping her arm through Tori's. She smiled at Nick and excused the giddiness she felt for weakness at not having eaten all day. "Let's go get this girl a fast-food fix."

They debated what to eat on the way over to Beach Burgers. Did they want a hamburger or cheeseburger, plain hot dog or chili dog? Tori thought she might even want a corn dog. Once there, however, burgers won out as the aroma drifted out to meet them. Nick handed Tori the money and sent her to order cheeseburgers and drinks for the three of them, while he led Meagan to a nearby outside table.

After pulling out a chair for Meagan, Nick took a seat next to her. The smallness of the table made him seem even larger, and Meagan found herself wondering if he had to have his jacket specially made for those shoulders.

When his elbow knocked against hers, she couldn't ignore the little tingles that shot up her arm. *Friends, huh? Friends don't feel tingles at a casual touch*, Meagan thought. Was friendship going to be possible? Suddenly, she wished she hadn't come. She felt as if she were cheating on Thad when she hadn't even accepted his proposal. Still, they had been seeing each other and—

"Meagan," Nick said, interrupting her thoughts, "look." He motioned toward the fast-food counter where Tori was waiting for their food. A young man was talking to her, and from the way he was looking at her and the way Tori responded, raising her hand to touch her hair, it seemed he was commenting on how nice she looked. Tori smiled at him, and her face glowed.

Nick reached over and took one of Meagan's hands in his own. "She's already showing more confidence in herself, Meagan. And she really likes you and she looks up to you. Thank you for taking the time for her today."

We're just friends, Meagan reminded herself, trying to ignore the sudden pounding of her heart as Nick gently squeezed her fingers. She pulled her hand back and slipped it in her lap. "You and your grandmother have done a wonderful job, Nick. Tori is a lovely young lady."

"Thank you. We've had a lot of help from the Lord, but it means a lot to me, to hear you say that."

Tori arrived with the food, a huge smile on her face. She'd no more than sat down when she asked, "Did you see him? Isn't he wonderful?"

"See whom?" Nick asked, looking at Meagan and winking. "Did you see anyone?"

"Well, there was that good-looking young man hovering over her." She grinned at Tori. "Is that whom you are talking about?"

Tori nodded, her eyes bright and her color high. "He

asked for my phone number!" she whispered.

"Are we supposed to know who he is, or are you going to let us in on it?" Nick's whisper was exaggerated.

Tori had just taken a bite of her burger and kept them waiting until she chewed and swallowed. "His name is Rod Williams, and he's in some of my classes, even though he's a junior. I sure would like to go to homecoming with him!"

"Oh. *That* boy," Nick growled. "How do you know I'd let you go with him, if he does ask?"

"Nicky!" Tori looked at him, her eyes wide and imploring. "I know I can't really date-date, yet. But, this is special. It's homecoming. Everyone goes to that!"

"*Everyone*, huh?" Nick asked.

"Well, all of my friends do." Tori let the subject drop and ate the rest of her meal with a dreamy look in her eyes.

Nick frowned, and Meagan had a feeling Tori was growing up way too fast for his comfort. She smiled and nudged his shoulder. "You aren't ready for all of this, are you?"

He shook his head and laughed. "No. I'm not."

"I don't think you have much choice," Meagan said gently as she nodded toward Tori. The teenager appeared not to have heard a word they were saying.

Nick glanced at his little sister before turning back to Meagan. "You're probably right about that, but I don't have to like it, do I?"

Meagan chuckled and shook her head. "No, you don't have to like it."

They spent the rest of the meal in silence, each one seemingly lost in thought, and when they'd finished eating they looked at one another and burst out laughing. "We might as well have eaten alone for all the company we've been to each other," Meagan said.

They were still laughing as they cleared their table and walked back to Meagan's shop.

Tori thanked Meagan once more and gave her a hug.

"Next time, we promise to be better company," Nick said before mouthing, "thank you," as he and Tori headed for his car.

When she reached the shop, Meagan was glad that customers kept her and Ronni busy enough to keep her friend and coworker from asking how dinner went with Nick and Tori. Meagan still wasn't sure about that friendship thing with Nick. She'd truly enjoyed eating with him and Tori more than she'd expected to, even during the quiet time at the table—and she didn't know if that was a good thing or not.

seven

Later that night, just as Meagan was getting ready for bed, the phone rang. Thinking it was Thad, she answered it eagerly.

Nick's husky voice greeted her. "Meagan? Look, I want to apologize for going into never-never land at dinner tonight."

Feeling a little relieved for reasons she didn't understand and certainly didn't want to think about, Meagan chuckled and propped herself up against the headboard with one of her pillows. "Nick, it's all right, really. My mind was a little busy, too. Did Rod call Tori?"

"He did," Nick growled. "He asked her to go to homecoming with him."

"Are you going to let her go?"

His sigh sounded deep, even over the phone line. "Yes, I guess. She's going to be sixteen soon, and I can't keep her under lock and key, I know. Meagan, I just hope I'm doing the right thing by letting her go."

Meagan couldn't help being touched by his concern about his little sister. "Nick, you are going to have to trust her sometime."

"It's not *her* I worry about," Nick said.

His voice sounded tense to her ears, but she couldn't help laughing. "It all comes back to haunt you, doesn't it?"

The tension seemed to break as Nick laughed, too. "You bet it does. I did tell her the only way she could go at all was to double-date."

"That was very wise." Meagan knew he was really concerned and sought to reassure him. "Nick, I'm sure Tori will be fine. She seems like she's got a good head on her shoulders."

Nick let out a long sigh. "Thanks, Meagan. I know she does, but I needed to hear it from someone else. All she's talked about all evening is this Rod person and you. Thank you again for this afternoon. Grams said to tell you that she might even be in for a makeover, you did such a good job on Tori."

"Your grandmother is a gem, Nick. You tell her it'd be hard to improve on her, but she's welcome to come in anytime."

"I'll be sure to tell her." There was silence for a moment before Nick spoke again. "Meagan?"

Something in the tone of his voice had Meagan's heart beating a little faster. "Yes, Nick?"

"Would you let me take you to dinner—a real one this time—to thank you for all you did for Tori today?"

"Nick, there's no need to—"

"Please, Meagan. You don't know how Grams and I have worked to try to help Tori feel good about herself. You managed to do that in one afternoon. I need to show you our appreciation. Besides, you go out with Jeff from time to time, don't you?"

"Well, yes, but—" *Jeff is like a brother to me, and there is Thad to think about. But Nick doesn't know about Thad. . .and Thad doesn't know about him.*

"You said we'd try to be friends."

He had her there. Meagan didn't know how to get around it when he put it that way. "All right, Nick. I'll have dinner with you."

"How's tomorrow night? You aren't working late, are you?"

She might as well agree. If she put it off, she'd only get more nervous than she was now. "Tomorrow night will work. What time?"

"How about seven? Is that all right?"

"Seven will be fine."

"Good. I'll see you then, Meagan. Good night."

"Night," Meagan said. She heard the click on the other end of the line, but she kept staring at the receiver. Why had she agreed to go out with him? She had no business going anywhere with Nick—not with Thad waiting for an answer to his proposal. Meagan finally hung up the phone and tried to change her train of thoughts.

All she and Nick were going to be was friends—and nothing more. That's what they both had agreed on, to try to be friends again. It would take a little while to get there, that's all.

In the meantime, she needed to quit thinking of Nick and think about Thad. He loved her and wanted to spend the rest of his life with her. And that's what she wanted, too—wasn't it? Suddenly she felt the need to talk to Thad, to picture his sweet smile and hear his voice. To tell him she was going to dinner with an old friend. Meagan reached for the phone and then jumped when it rang. She lifted the receiver. "Hello?"

As if he could read her thoughts from long distance, it was Thad. "Hi, love. I miss you."

"Thad. I was just thinking about you." *And how awful I feel that I don't think of you enough.*

"I wanted to see how things are going and tell you that I love you."

"Things are going really well at the shop."

"That's wonderful. And I'm really glad for you. I just wish you were back here with me."

"I know. But, Thad, remember that I said I might stay on until after Christmas. I may be able to come back for a week or so, but the shop in Dallas is doing just fine and right now I'm needed here." Still she felt a need to see this man who cared so much about her. "Why don't you come down for a weekend? Do you think you could get away?"

"I wish I could. I've just started work on the advertising campaign for that new chain of hotels I told you about. I received the go-ahead from them today."

"Oh, Thad, that's great! I'm so happy for you." Meagan had to think hard to remember the company he was talking about. Suddenly, she realized she wasn't being fair to this man. He deserved an answer to his proposal and her undivided attention when she was talking to him—and her loyalty and honesty.

"Maybe I can come down in a few weeks."

"That would be wonderful." She needed to see him, to focus on the relationship they had when she left Dallas. Some said that absence made the heart grow fonder, but Meagan had a feeling *they* didn't know what they were talking about.

"Have you been catching up with your old crowd?"

"Some. I've been too busy to do much." Meagan felt the pull to be honest with him. "I was talked into going out to dinner with the friend whose law firm has handled things for me here in Mississippi."

"Oh?"

"Yes. I helped his little sister today, and he wants to repay me." Meagan didn't wait for Thad's reaction to that and hurried on with, "I've had several friends come in for consultations, but I haven't had time for much socializing. What have you been doing?"

Thad chuckled. "Working and missing you."

"I'm sorry, Thad. I—"

"It's all right, Meagan. You didn't know I was going to ask you to marry me when you made plans to open a new shop in your hometown. I do understand that your energies have to go into that right now. I can be patient awhile longer."

"Thad. . ." Meagan suddenly felt like crying. This man was so sweet and she was—

"I will be down there soon. I can wait for your answer, but I want to see you just as soon as I can."

"I want to see you, too." Meagan *needed* to see him. When she left Dallas, she was pretty sure what her answer to his proposal was going to be. But now she knew she had to see Thad again—and even then she wasn't sure she'd know what her answer would be. *Dear Lord, please help me to know what to do.*

&

Nick sat at his desk in the study, staring at the phone for several minutes before letting out a big whoop. He couldn't believe Meagan had agreed to go out with him. Of course, he hadn't given her much of a chance to say no. He knew bringing up her friendship with Jeff like that wasn't very fair, but he was thankful it had worked. *Thank You, Lord.*

And he knew he wasn't really being honest in pretending that he only wanted them to be friends. Oh, yes, he wanted that—but he wanted more. He knew now that he was falling in love with Meagan all over again, only now as the warm, wonderful woman she'd turned into. He just wanted the chance to win her love once more—this time for good. But Nick knew he had to go slow, or she'd turn and run the other way before he ever had a chance to get her to fall in love with him again. He'd do well to remember that.

He'd had such a good time with her and Tori today, and he was really looking forward to taking her to dinner tomorrow night. He knew she didn't think of it as a date, but he hoped that before the night was over, she might. Nick sighed. If not—then he'd just have to pray for patience.

Nick turned out all the lights downstairs and took the steps two at a time. The box was sitting on his bed. Grams had told him she'd found it. Now he sat down on the side of his bed and opened it, peering down at its contents.

He smiled back at the picture he lifted out of the box. It was a five-by-seven of Meagan, a little younger than Tori was now. She'd been a pretty girl, showing a hint of the beautifully mature woman she'd become.

Nick rummaged through the box until he found what he was looking for. His hand closed around the glass ornament Meagan had given him for Christmas, and he brought it out to catch the light. He was glad he'd kept it all this time. He brought out another picture. This was a snapshot taken that Christmas, right after he and Meagan had exchanged gifts. Nick traced the two people in the photograph. Had they really been so young?

He sighed. Yes. They had been that young—too young. And that had been the problem. He put everything back in the box and took it to his closet, feeling sad about the past as he slid the box onto a shelf. Yet, there was the future, and maybe another chance for them. Only time would tell.

❧

"Just friends, huh?" Ronni asked the next afternoon as Meagan first forgot her purse then her briefcase before heading upstairs. "Meagan, I don't think I've ever seen you so nervous."

Meagan dropped back down into her chair. "Oh, Ronni. It's just that part of me doesn't want to go out with Nick tonight, and the other part does. I just feel so confused about everything."

Ronni perched on the edge of Meagan's desk. "Why? Because of Thad, or because of the past?"

Meagan took a deep breath. "Yes and no. I mean. . .a lot of years have passed since we went together in high school. I don't really know this Nick. I mean, I did know him, but now—and there is Thad. He asked me to marry him right before I came down here to open the shop."

"Oh. I didn't know your relationship was that serious."

"I'm sorry, Ronni. I haven't told anyone about the proposal except my family and now—you. I'm not sure. . ." She shook her head and looked up at her friend. "I haven't given him my answer yet. And—I'm not making any sense, am I?"

Ronni smiled at her. "Not much, but go on. Maybe I can figure it out."

Meagan wasn't even sure she wanted it sorted out. She glanced at her watch and jumped up. Waving her hand limply, she said, "I don't have time to go into it all right now. It's all right. It's just a case of confusion. I'll be fine."

"Are you sure?" Ronni asked.

Meagan saw the look of concern on Ronni's face and patted her shoulder. "I'm sure."

"Okay." Ronni nodded. "But if you need to talk, I'm here."

Meagan suddenly felt selfish. So much had been going on in her life lately that she hadn't really shown much concern about Ronni. "How are things going with you? I know it's been very tough for you and Claudia."

Ronni smiled and shrugged. "We're doing all right. I love working for you, and Claudia is concentrating on helping Magnolia Bay come back to life. She's determined that the casinos aren't going to do any more damage to the people and place she loves. We'll be okay. The Lord will get us through."

"I think you can be fairly certain of that," Meagan said as she hugged her friend, "thankfully."

28

Meagan recalled the conversation as she got ready for dinner with Nick. Her worries were nothing compared to Ronni losing her husband at such an early age. *Dear Lord, please be with Ronni and Claudia and comfort them as only You can. They've both been through so much. Please let me help them in whatever way I can, too.*

Feeling unsettled about the evening, she sighed as she brushed out her hair and let it curl around her face. Her hand trembled as she applied a last coat of mascara. She *was* nervous. Why? She knew Nick. It wasn't as if he were someone new in her life. Or was it? She'd known the young, brash Nick—not the man he was now. Meagan liked this man, or at least what she'd seen of him so far. The past was over. Nick had asked for her forgiveness, and she'd given it to him. He wanted her friendship, and she realized she wanted his, too. There was no reason for her to feel nervous. She was just going out to dinner with a friend.

But when the doorbell rang, she didn't stop to ask herself why her heart felt as if it might jump out of her chest. She took a deep breath and hurried to answer the door.

Nick stood there grinning down at her, looking wonderful in a suit and tie. His glance slid over her. "I like that dress. You look beautiful."

As Nick's gaze rested on her, she was glad she'd decided on the pure teal jacket dress that was one of her favorites. She'd learned long ago that, when she was nervous, it helped her comfort level to wear something she felt really good in.

"Thank you, Nick. You don't look so bad, yourself."

"Thanks." He laughed, and Meagan thought he even turned a little red at her compliment. "Anywhere in particular you'd like to go?"

Meagan smiled at him and shook her head. "I've been away a long time, Nick. You choose."

❧

Nick suddenly felt like a teenager on his first date, tongue-tied and wanting desperately to please this lovely woman. Meagan gathered her purse, and Nick was thankful for the chance to give himself a pep talk. She'd only agreed to try to be friends. This wasn't a date to her, and he needed to remember that.

Meagan turned back to him. "So? Where are we going?"

"We'll try Mike's place, if that's all right with you. I feel like we ought to support the new businesses in town."

"That's fine with me. I hear the food is only getting better." Her smile as she glanced up assured Nick that she was totally unaware of the way she could make his heart swell.

He wondered why that surprised him. Meagan had never truly realized the effect she had on others. Many years had passed, and she'd been gone a long time. It was just hard to believe that she'd been able to keep that particularly endearing quality, yet it appeared that she had.

Their conversation on the way to the restaurant was mostly one-sided, as Meagan commented on some of the changes that had taken place while she was gone, but Nick didn't mind. He loved hearing her voice.

"Do you think Magnolia Bay will ever make a real comeback?"

"Well, with you and Mike and the others trying so hard to make it happen, I certainly hope so. I know the town did the right thing by refusing to let casinos in here, but it's paid a heavy price. Still, I have to believe there are tourists who don't want any part of the gambling scene and will welcome a slower pace. We just have to find a way to let them know about Magnolia Bay. I do think it's going to take time."

Meagan nodded. "I agree. I just hope we didn't all wait too long to try to bring it back."

Nick pulled into the Seaside Surf and Turf's parking lot and found a space not far from the entrance. He turned the engine off and went around to open Meagan's door.

She gracefully stepped out of the car and turned to him, letting out a huge sigh. "Oh, Nick. It feels so good to be home."

He looked into her shining eyes and wished that part of her happiness at being back could be credited to being with him. For now, though, he would content himself with the fact that she *was* with him, and with how happy *he* was to have her home.

"It's wonderful to have you here, Meagan." He put his hand to her back and led the way into the restaurant. *And I hope you never leave again.*

❧

Meagan admired the warm décor with bronze ceiling tiles and the different dining levels. She wondered why she hadn't noticed them the night of the get-together with her old group. She must have been too apprehensive to notice much of anything that night.

They were seated at a corner table that overlooked both Bay Drive Bridge and the bay itself. There was a casual, yet intimate feel to the restaurant. Her stomach fluttered when she realized this was really the first real date she'd ever had with Nick. Because she'd been too young at fourteen to officially date, their "dates" had been limited to only a few afternoon movies with several other kids or running to a fast-food restaurant for a hamburger. This, on the other hand, was exactly the kind of place they'd gone to in her daydreams. Meagan pulled herself up short. This wasn't a date. She reminded herself that it was only dinner with a friend.

Nick smiled at her as the waiter left them menus and went to get the iced tea they'd ordered. "This is a really nice place, isn't it? I think Mike is going to do well here."

Meagan nodded. "I do, too." She glanced out the window and chuckled. "I see some things never change."

Nick looked outside and saw what she was talking about. Teenagers occupied at least two-thirds of the passing vehicles. He nodded. "You are right. Bay Drive is still the main drag."

"Scary, now, isn't it?" Meagan asked.

Nick shuddered slightly. "I'm just glad Tori doesn't have her driver's license yet."

Meagan tried to hold back the giggle that escaped and couldn't help grinning. "I'm sorry, Nick. It's just nice to see how responsible you are toward Tori. She seems like a fine young lady."

He leaned back in his chair and grinned at her. He had the nicest smile. She had to concentrate on his next words.

"Surprised that I managed to mature a little, are you? Don't feel bad, Meagan. No one was more stunned than I was when I began to show a little responsibility. On the other hand, it doesn't surprise me at all that you've turned into a beautiful, mature woman. The promise of all you've become was there when you were young."

Meagan felt the warm color flood her face at Nick's compliment, and suddenly she didn't feel like a mature woman anymore. She felt young and confused and was very relieved when the waiter came to take their order.

She ordered the shrimp étouffée and Nick ordered the blackened redfish, both classic Cajun dishes from neighboring Louisiana. Nick added an onion mum as an appetizer.

"I'm sure everything is going to be wonderful, but when did Mike do away with the all-you-can-eat bar?" Meagan asked.

"He only does that for groups and special parties. He wanted the restaurant to be more than just a 'serve yourself' place."

Meagan nodded as she looked around. "The atmosphere is really nice. And it's nice to have sit-down service."

"Yes. I like Doug's Restaurant over in Gulfport, too. It's fairly new and a bit louder, but the food is very good. We'll have to try it sometime."

Meagan's heartbeat skittered at his words, and she told herself there shouldn't be a next time. Yet she found herself hoping there would be. She liked being with Nick—she always had.

"What made you want to go into color consulting, Meagan?" Nick asked, seemingly out of the blue.

"Oh, I don't know. I've always been intrigued by how

colors could either enhance or detract from one's natural beauty. I believe the Lord has given special qualities to everyone, inside and out. It's so rewarding to see a woman's confidence blossom when she knows she looks her best and to know I've helped her feel better about herself."

"I know Tori has a different, more confident air about her since you worked with her. She seems to be wearing less makeup, too. How did you do that?"

Meagan chuckled. "I didn't; not really. She just doesn't need it when she wears the colors that are right for her. Besides, she's got that wonderful young skin that just glows with health and youth. It was really fun to work with her."

"Look for more of her friends to make appointments with you. She's told everyone she knows how wonderful you are. She thinks you are her special expert."

"How sweet! I hope she feels she can consult with me anytime."

Talk turned to old friends and what had been going on in each of their lives during the past ten years and continued after the waiter brought their appetizer and set it on the table. Caught up in their conversation, they'd barely made a dent in the huge deep-fried onion when Nick's name was called, loudly.

❧

Nick looked up to see Darla Jenkins heading toward them, and he groaned inwardly. Meagan smiled graciously at the other woman as she approached their table, but Darla appeared not to have seen her at all and walked straight up to him as if he were the only one at the table.

"Nick! I was beginning to worry that you were sick. You haven't returned any of my calls."

Had she always sounded so whiny? Nick wondered. *Or*

was it a new trait she'd acquired? "I'm sorry, Darla. I've been really busy," Nick said. And that was the truth, but it wasn't the reason he hadn't returned her calls. He felt bad, but he'd found that he and Darla had nothing at all in common, and he just wasn't interested in going out with her again. "You remember Meagan Evans, don't you?"

"Yes, of course." Darla gave Meagan tight smile before turning her attention back to Nick. "I hope things are slowing down now, and we'll be able to get together soon."

Nick didn't know how to tell her that he didn't plan on going out with her again, but even if he found a way, somehow he didn't think that would keep her from calling him. "I'm sorry, Darla. I—"

Darla's hand reached out to rub his arm. "It's all right, Nicky. I know how hard you work. I just wanted to check on you and see how you are doing. Remember we left the reunion thing because you weren't feeling well."

"I'm fine, now. Thanks for asking." Nick didn't know what to say next. He just wanted the woman to leave them alone. He hadn't missed the different expressions that passed over Meagan's face. She seemed curious at first, then a little disgusted, and finally, now, she didn't seem to want to meet his eyes, as if she didn't trust him. He'd seen that look before and was sure that the past had raised its ugly head once more in her mind.

Darla wrapped her arms around his neck and leaned in close. "Call me, Nicky."

Nick felt his own disgust rising as he firmly disengaged her arms. "Darla, I think your friends are leaving."

Only then did she turn to the friends she'd probably told to wait on her. "I guess you're right. You call, you hear?"

Nick breathed a sigh of relief when she walked off.

He looked over at Meagan. "I'm really sorry about that, Meagan." From the look on her face, Nick had a feeling any progress he might have made just exited right along with Darla.

&

Meagan had been thinking about the past and for a moment, when Darla walked up, she'd even felt the hurt of the past again. But that was before she read the pleading look Nick had given her just now. He hadn't known how to handle the situation any more than she would have.

Besides, what right did she have to be upset? Nick had been living his life before she came back into it, the same as she had. She hadn't even told him about Thad or his proposal. Nick certainly didn't owe her an explanation. The past was the past. This was the present, and she didn't want anything to spoil the fragile thread of friendship they'd begun to weave tonight.

"Don't worry about it, Nick."

Nick shook his head. "I just don't know what to say."

"You don't have to say anything. Just tell me if I'm causing a problem for you by being out with you." Maybe she'd read him wrong and there was something going on between him and Darla.

It seemed to take a moment for what she was asking to register with Nick. "You mean with Darla?"

Meagan nodded.

"No. Meagan, I've only had one date with the woman, and that was to Mike's opening that night."

Meagan held her hand up to stop him as soon as the first 'no' was out, but he continued. "I've talked to her a few times when we've run into each other, but that's all. Really."

"Nick, you don't owe me any explanation." And he didn't,

but she felt an immense sense of relief that he wasn't involved with Darla. "I just don't want to cause you any problems."

"You're not," he said shortly.

"Nick," Meagan said softly, "this isn't the past. We aren't continuing an old relationship; we're supposed to be beginning a new friendship, right?"

When Nick met her eyes, he smiled and said, "Right."

"And so far it's going pretty well, wouldn't you say?" Meagan waited for Nick to answer, liking the smile in his eyes even before it reached his mouth.

"I'd say it's going very—"

Meagan's cell phone went off at that moment and stopped Nick from finishing what he was going to say as she pulled it out and answered it.

"Hello?"

"Meagan?" It was Thad. The sound of his voice reminded her that she shouldn't even be concerned about who Nick was seeing. "I tried your home, but there was no answer. I had the feeling you were a little down last night when we talked, and I wanted to make sure you are all right."

"I'm fine, Thad."

"You sound a little stressed now. Are you sure—"

"I'll be fine, Thad. I promise." And she prayed that she would be. She just couldn't tell him she wasn't stressed, because if talking to the man who was waiting for her answer to his proposal while having dinner with her old love wasn't a little stressful, she didn't know what would be.

"I can cancel my trip and come down there, if you need me to."

"No. That's not necessary. This account is important to you. Just come down in a few weeks, if you can."

"I'll be there. I don't like us being apart, Meagan."

"I know—"

Just then the waiter came with their meal.

"Where are you? Have I interrupted you?"

"It's okay. I'm having dinner out, and the waiter just brought the food," Meagan said, keeping her eyes on the plate set in front of her, instead of looking at Nick.

"Oh! I'm sorry. Is this the night you were going out with your old friend?"

"Yes."

"I'm sorry. I'll let you go then. I just wanted to see how you were and tell you that I love you."

"Thank you, Thad."

"I'll talk to you later. Night, Meagan."

"Good night." She sighed inwardly as Thad hung up on his end and she flipped down her phone and slid it back into her purse.

"Mmm, this looks wonderful," said Meagan, hoping Nick wouldn't ask her about the phone call.

"I don't think I've heard you mention a Thad before."

Obviously, she wasn't going to get her wish. Naturally he would be curious. "No? He's the one who created the advertising campaign for Meagan's Color Cottage. We became acquainted that way, and then we found we attend the same church in Dallas."

"Are you dating him?"

Meagan was almost relieved to answer honestly. "Yes. We've been seeing each other."

"I see." Nick nodded.

No, he didn't. Not really. Because as much as Meagan knew she should tell him that Thad had proposed to her and was waiting for her answer, she couldn't bring herself to say the words. Instead, she forced herself to take a bite from her plate and changed the subject after she chewed and swallowed. "This is really good. How is yours?"

Nick seemed to be deep in thought, but he took a bite and nodded. "It's very good."

They concentrated on their meals in silence for a few minutes before starting a new conversation about food that took them through the rest of the meal.

Meagan didn't feel like dessert—her stomach was churning in a way that had nothing to do with what she'd eaten, and she was more confused than ever about her feelings for both Thad and Nick. She glanced at her watch and wasn't sure if she was thankful or sad that the evening was almost over. "I didn't realize it was getting so late. I guess maybe we ought to be going."

"Let's have one more cup of coffee, and then we'll go."

Meagan quickly agreed, realizing that she wasn't ready to be alone with all of her thoughts just yet. The waiter came to refill their cups, and Meagan sat back in her chair, glad that Nick wasn't ready for the evening to end yet, either.

This had been so nice—catching up with everything and getting to know each other again. Well, most of the evening had been nice. All accept for the Darla incident and the phone call from Thad. The timing of both had not been the best, but maybe it was going to be possible for her and Nick to be friends after all.

When Nick reached over and picked up one of her hands in his, she almost forgot to breathe, and Meagan had to remind herself that friendship was what they were working on—nothing more.

"I've enjoyed this so much, Meagan. I hope you did, too."

Oh, yes, she'd enjoyed it. As her heartbeat sped up, she

wondered if she might have enjoyed it too much. "I had a wonderful time, Nick."

"I'm glad. It was the least I could do after all you did for Tori."

Meagan drew her hand away, suddenly feeling hurt. Had he only taken her out because he felt he owed her—because of Tori? Was that the only reason for this evening?

"You don't owe me anything, Nick. I told you how much I enjoyed helping Tori. And I believe you spent quite a lot in my shop because of all my help."

Nick grinned at her. "That's true. I guess maybe it's you who owes me."

Meagan's good mood suddenly evaporated. She didn't want them to be together because one "owed" the other. And yet. . .she shouldn't be wanting them to be together at all. She was practically engaged to another man. What was wrong with her?

They walked to the car in silence, but when he opened the door for her, Nick touched her on the shoulder and asked, "Meagan, are you all right?"

"I'm fine, Nick." How could she tell him she wasn't sure they could ever be friends like he wanted? She was way too attracted to him, too aware of him—of his strong hands gripping the steering wheel, the scent of his aftershave. The car seemed too small, and he seemed too close. She was much too attracted to him to think of him as a friend.

The drive back to her apartment seemed longer than the one to the restaurant had, especially when Nick tuned the radio to an oldies station and Nat King Cole's "Unforgettable" began to play. She was beginning to realize the feelings she'd always felt for Nick were just that—unforgettable. Both the good *and* the bad, and she didn't know how to get past it all and on to the friendship Nick said he wanted now.

When Nick suddenly changed the radio station she wondered if he was thinking along the same lines. At her apartment, she didn't wait for him to open the car door for her, but did wait for him to walk her to her front door. When she fumbled with the keys, he took them from her and easily unlocked the door.

Before she could even wonder whether he expected to be asked in, he lifted her chin so that she was looking into his warm brown eyes.

"You're sure you are all right?" he asked.

Meagan chewed her bottom lip and nodded. She was—except that she had the sudden urge to cry at his gentle concern. "I'm sure."

"Thank you for going with me tonight. I really enjoyed it."

Meagan nodded. "So did I. Thank you."

He smiled down at her and inclined his head. Meagan had never thought of herself as a coward until now. She turned her face so that Nick's lips softly brushed her cheek then backed into her apartment. "Good night, Nick."

"Good night, Meagan. I'll be in touch." Nick turned and walked down the stairs.

eight

Still too keyed up over the events of the evening, Meagan got ready for bed but found she wasn't ready to go to sleep. She made a cup of hot tea, settled in her recliner, and turned on an old movie. She tried to concentrate on it long enough to get interested in it—or sleepy enough to go to bed—but thoughts of Nick and Thad warred with each other until she finally gave up and slipped out onto her balcony.

Pulling her housecoat a little tighter around her as the cooling breeze came off the water and gave a tiny hint of fall, Meagan finally gave in to letting herself think about the evening she and Nick had just shared. She'd enjoyed his company and the whole night more than she'd thought possible. Their conversation over dinner had revealed more of the man as they'd played catch-up.

He'd listened while she talked, asking questions, chuckling at some of her funny stories, and giving her his full attention.

Nick had her laughing at stories of his college days and wanting to cry as he briefly went into the deaths of his father and grandfather. She'd been impressed with how dedicated he was to keeping his family's name one to be proud of in the community.

It couldn't have been easy to take over one of the best-known law firms in the area, not to mention becoming the head of his family. He'd been so young for such enormous responsibility. It had to have been hard on him, but he was clearly comfortable with the responsibility now.

Meagan liked Nick—really liked him. He seemed to have become, in reality, what she'd dreamed he would be when they'd been young. He had grown into a kind, caring man who loved his family dearly.

No, he didn't appear to be the same boy she'd cared about once; and it was entirely possible that he was a man she could fall in love with all over again—if she hadn't already. And there lay the danger—heartbreak all over again if Nick didn't return her feelings. And where did that leave Thad? She knew firsthand how horrible is was to have her heart broken. How could she break his? She didn't even know what to pray for so she simply whispered, "Dear Lord, please help me. I don't know what to do."

⁂

Nick sat in his study with his hand poised over the phone. He shook his head and rubbed that same hand over his eyes. No. Now was not the time to call Meagan. He needed to go slow and steady if he ever hoped to have a future with her.

And he did want that future, even if it meant they'd only be friends. He'd be lying to himself if he said that's all he wanted to settle for. Tonight proved to him that the feelings he'd always had for her were deepening each time he saw her.

Up until Darla interrupted their evening, it had gone better than he'd expected. They'd had fun catching each other up on their lives. Meagan had him laughing frequently with her stories of starting up her own business. And she'd been a wonderful listener. Even after Darla showed up, things might have gone all right—until that Thad person called her. After that, there had been a definite damper on the evening.

Had Meagan been thinking of the man she'd been dating

and comparing him to Nick? Maybe she'd been remembering their past again. Nick certainly hadn't been trustworthy as a young man; why should she think he had changed? Maybe she thought the past would repeat itself. But she had no reason to believe that yet, and he planned to keep it that way. They were nothing more than friends at the moment—much as he'd like it to be different.

If he had anything to do with it, things *would* be different. Meagan had more than lived up to her youthful promise—she'd known from the beginning what she wanted to do with her life, and she'd planned, worked hard, and saved, never losing sight of her goal. Somehow, she'd managed to keep her faith, her sweetness and sense of humor, and her optimistic outlook on life at the same time. She was a woman worth going after even with this Thad person in the picture—especially with him in the picture. She wasn't wearing an engagement ring, and she was here. Time might be running out, and Nick couldn't give up without at least trying to convince Meagan he was a changed man.

And he was determined to do just that. It was up to him to prove to her that he had changed for the better and that he would treasure her love forever—if he were fortunate enough to win it back. *Dear Lord, I can only do it with Your help. Please guide me in this. I truly believe Meagan and I are meant to be together. If I'm wrong, please let me know. In Jesus' name, amen.*

❧

Ronni was off the next day, and Meagan was glad. She didn't want to have to give her friend an account of the night before—especially when she still didn't know how she felt about it.

It was a busy day, with several consultations scheduled

and new stock to check in, and she tried to concentrate on the jobs at hand instead of thinking about Nick's smile or the softness of his lips on her cheek. Then she'd think about Thad and feel horrible that her thoughts were on Nick instead of him.

Still, she kept hoping Nick would call and then wondered what she'd say if he did. When the afternoon and evening had passed without Meagan hearing from him, she told herself it appeared he really hadn't changed that much. He'd done this when they were in high school—saying he'd call, but he wouldn't.

Remembering their conversation at the end of the evening last night, she admitted that he hadn't said he would call her. Only that he'd be in touch. And he didn't say when. Meagan sighed and went to meet her last appointment for the day. She *had* to quit thinking about Nick.

By the time she called it a day and headed upstairs to her apartment, she was totally aggravated with herself. Her mood didn't get any better when she heard the phone ringing, but by the time she reached it and picked up the receiver it had stopped. Sighing with frustration, she went directly to the kitchen to put the water on to boil. She was glad she'd worked late tonight, because it gave her less time to mope around the apartment.

It was only after she'd brewed a cup of tea and sat down to go through her mail that she noticed the answering machine light was blinking and that there were two messages.

The first one was from Thad. She had to smile when she heard his voice, saying, "Hi, Meagan, my love, I'm sorry I missed you. I just wanted to let you know that I'll be down there as soon as I can get this campaign proposal finished.

I miss you. I can't wait to see you. If it's not too late when you get this message, give me a call, okay?"

He deserved that much from her, Meagan thought as she dialed his number. He was so sweet, and she did care deeply for him. *But do I really love him enough to marry him?* His answering machine picked up just then, and she couldn't help feeling a little relieved, both because she didn't have time to answer her own question and because she wasn't sure what to say to him. It wasn't easy to even leave him a message.

"Thad, it's me. I'm sorry I wasn't in when you called. I worked late tonight. I know you'll do a wonderful job with that ad campaign you are working on. . .and. . .I'll be looking for you when you get time to come down here. You take care, you hear?"

It was only when she hung up that she realized she hadn't told him she missed him and wondered why she hadn't. Quickly deleting his message, Meagan remembered that she had another message, and she punched the PLAY button on her machine once more. Her heart took a triple tumble when she heard Nick's voice.

"Meagan, I tried to call you at work, but I must have missed you by only minutes. They said you'd just left. I wanted to let you know that I'm about to get on a plane headed for Jackson. Something has come up that I need to take care of. I'll try to call you while I'm gone, but in case I miss you, I wanted to let you know that Grams will be bringing Tori in to find something to wear for homecoming sometime this week. I know you'll help her find something that she *and* I both can live with."

He chuckled next, and Meagan's heart went out to him as he continued. "Can you tell I am not ready for all of this?

Anyway, I just wanted to touch base with you. I should be home in a few days, and I hope we can get together for dinner when I get back. I hope you had a good day. You take care and don't work too hard."

The answering machine clicked off, but Meagan couldn't bring herself to erase the message.

Suddenly, she didn't feel quite so lonely or so tired. She finished looking at her mail and drinking her tea, in a much better frame of mind. Meagan went to take a shower, humming all the way down the hall.

It was nice to have someone ask about her day and tell her to take care of herself. Someone to let her know he was thinking about her. Someone who had kept in touch, just like he said he would. Thad did those very same things, but for some reason, it just didn't feel the same. Maybe it was because Nick had kept his word. Or maybe it was because she'd been away from Thad for too long. Meagan didn't know. She only knew that it was Nick's message that had her smiling each time she replayed it that night.

ఎ

Meagan's good mood carried over to the next day. Even Ronni commented on it. "I haven't heard you hum in a long time. What is that song?"

Having stopped midhum as Ronni began talking, Meagan had to think about what it was she was humming to.

"Oh, it's 'Unforgettable' isn't it? I love that song, but I haven't heard it in ages," Ronni said, putting a name to the tune before Meagan had a chance to realize what it was.

Neither had I, Meagan thought. Not until Nick came back into her life. Now she'd been humming the tune and hearing the words over and over again.

"You're certainly in a good mood today," Ronni said. "Does it have anything to do with Nick? Or"—she looked confused as she finished—"maybe Thad? I'm sorry, Meagan. I sound quite nosy, don't I? You don't have to answer."

Meagan was sure that Ronni only had her best interests at heart and meant no harm by her questions. "It's okay. I had a message from both last night. Thad says he'll be here soon as he can get away. And Nick. . ." Well, Nick certainly was connected to the mood and the song, but Meagan was glad to be able to answer honestly, if evasively. "I think he's out of town."

She almost chuckled at the disappointed look Ronni gave her, feeling a little guilty that she wasn't being completely open with her friend, although nothing had really happened between her and Nick to report on. He'd called and left a message. That was all. And like the teenager she used to be, it had made her night—and her day.

When one of Ronni's consulting appointments came in, Meagan was relieved not to have to talk about Nick anymore, and she could escape to the back to check in new merchandise that had come in earlier in the day.

Concentrating on her work, she jumped when the buzzer suddenly sounded in the stockroom. It'd been installed to alert her, or whoever was working in the back, that they were needed up front, but it was rarely used. Now she hurried to see if there was a problem and was pleasantly surprised to find her mother had come in to ask her to lunch.

Once they received their order from Beach Burgers and found a table, Meagan found it wasn't quite as easy to avoid her mom's questions as it had been Ronni's.

"How did your dinner out with Nick go, honey?" Jenny

asked as they took their plates off the trays and got ready to enjoy their meal.

"It was fine."

"Fine? Nothing else?"

Meagan chuckled. Her mom had always been direct and able to read her well. It was probably one reason they'd always been close. There was no sense hiding anything from her.

"It was really enjoyable, Mom. He seems to have changed, to be more responsible. Remember, it was just a dinner to thank me for helping Tori. That's all."

Her mother looked closely at her, but all she said was, "Hmm. I'm glad you had a good time. Have you heard from Thad?"

Meagan almost choked on the sip of iced tea she'd just taken. Her mother certainly was curious today. "Yes, I had a message from him. He's going to try to get down here soon."

Her mother nodded. "That's good. We'd love to see him again. He's a good man."

"I know." Meagan changed the subject. "Are you all packed and ready to go to Arkansas?" Her parents and uncle were going to a family reunion, but Meagan didn't feel she could leave her new shop for more than a day off just yet.

Her mom nodded and swallowed the bite of French fry she'd just taken before speaking. "All packed. I wish you were going with us, but maybe you'll be able to go to the next one. Sure you'll be all right while we are gone?"

Meagan laughed. "Mom, I've lived away from you for years. I think I'll survive a week."

"I know you will. But I've gotten used to talking to you— if not seeing you—every day or so. It's so good to have you closer to us, even if only for a while."

"It is good to be nearer to you and Dad. Don't worry while you're gone. I'll be fine."

They spent the rest of the meal talking about the reunion and who all would be there. Meagan was glad her mother hadn't asked any more about Thad or Nick. It was hard enough trying not to let Ronni know her feelings were in turmoil over the two of them, and she wouldn't be able to hide it from her mother for very long, but at least she had a reprieve for a little while.

❧

Her mother had some shopping to do for the trip, so Meagan left her at her car outside the shop and went back inside Meagan's Color Cottage to find Tori and her grandmother waiting for her.

"Tori and Mrs. Chambers, how nice to see you again!"

"Hi, Mi—Meagan." Tori managed to cut off the "Miss" as Meagan had requested and grinned at her. "Did Nicky tell you we would be in?"

"He did." Meagan nodded and smiled at the excited teen. Tori's grin was contagious, and Meagan remembered how important homecomings were at that age. Actually, she'd be excited even now, to be asked to homecoming. Especially if a certain someone asked. But that wasn't going to happen.

"I really want to look nice for Rod. I still can't quite believe he asked me!"

Meagan remembered feeling that way when she was young, but she hurried to assure Tori that Rod was the lucky one.

"I'm sure Rod is having a hard time believing that *you* actually said you'd go with him!"

Tori blushed and grinned.

"Have you got an idea what you would like to wear? Are you thinking dressy or casual?"

"Well, some girls do really dress up for it, but most of my friends go kind of casual dressy. I'd just like to look nice—and be comfortable for the game and the party afterward."

After trying on several skirts, pants, and lightweight sweaters, and even some dresses, Tori decided on a deep purple skirt and matching jacket.

"Oh, that's got to be it, Tori," her grandmother said. "It looks wonderful on you."

"You look lovely, Tori," Meagan added, seeing the sparkle in the young girl's eyes. "Have you decided how to wear your hair?"

"I'm just going with the French braid and tucking it up at the back. It makes me feel more confident or something." Tori chuckled and shrugged.

"It makes her look older," Mrs. Chambers said, grinning at her granddaughter. She chuckled. "I'm not sure Nick is happy about that."

"Nicky is overprotective sometimes," Tori said, "but he's been responsible for me for a long time so I guess it's okay."

Meagan was impressed by the young girl's insight into her brother. They spent another half hour picking out accessories to go with the dress, and Meagan had such a good time helping them, she almost hated to see them leave.

One of Tori's friends came in to make a consultation appointment for the next day, and Nick's sister seemed proud to introduce her to Meagan.

The two girls began talking about homecoming, and Mrs. Chambers pulled Meagan to the side. "Thank you so much for helping Tori finally feel good about the way she looks, Meagan. Nick and I are so thrilled with the change in her, and we owe it all to you."

"Oh, Mrs. Chambers, you don't owe me anything. That's why I went into this business in the first place—to help women look their best. And I've gotten a special joy from helping Tori. She's a wonderful young lady."

"We certainly think so. Still, I want to thank you. With Nick out of town, we get a little lonesome at suppertime. I promised Tori we could eat at the Beach Burger tonight, and friends have asked us to eat with them tomorrow night, but won't you join us on Thursday night?"

Ronni was scheduled to close the shop that night, and it would be no problem for Meagan to leave early. It would be nice to have dinner with someone other than herself, and Mrs. Chambers seemed determined to do something for her. "I'd love to. Thank you so much. What time should I be there?"

"How about six thirty? Or is that too early?"

Meagan shook her head. "No. That's just right."

"Good. Dress casual."

Meagan nodded. "I will. Thank you, Mrs. Chambers."

Nick's grandmother shook her head. "No. Thank you. Tori, dear, I'm getting a little hungry. We need to be going."

"I'm ready, Grams." She turned to wave at Meagan. "Thank you so much for helping me, Meagan."

Tori's friend left the store with them, and Meagan went back to the storeroom looking forward to Thursday night.

Her last consultation of the day was with her high school friend Kay. Meagan had talked to her on the phone several times but hadn't seen her since the get-together at the Seaside Surf and Turf she went to with Jeff.

As was usual with their relationship, they quickly picked

up where they'd left off.

"I figured that as busy as we both are, possibly the easiest way to have a chat and catch up was if I came in," Kay said as she gave Meagan a quick hug.

Meagan showed Kay to a mirrored cubicle, pulled out her color swatches, and began to try different groups around Kay's neck. It didn't take long to figure out she was a Warm Fall, just as Meagan suspected. With her ivory skin tone and golden brown hair, she looked wonderful in the warm colors she almost always wore.

"Kay, you seem to have a natural instinct for what works best for you," Meagan said as she draped fall colors around her friend's neck. "You've always worn the right ones. You really didn't need to come to me for advice. That moss green you have on is perfect for you."

Kay chuckled. "Thank you, Meagan! I was hoping I was doing it right."

Meagan looked at her watch. "It's about break time for me. Let's grab a cup of coffee and go upstairs so I can show you my apartment."

"Sounds good to me," Kay said.

Meagan let Ronni know where she'd be, and she and Kay went upstairs.

"This is adorable, Meagan."

Meagan gave Kay a quick tour of the apartment; then they went out on the balcony to enjoy their coffee.

"How is business doing?" Kay asked. "I know it can be touch and go just starting out. At least that's how it was with mine."

"Better than I expected, actually," Meagan said. "Lately, most of my clients have been teenagers, thanks to Nick's sister, Tori."

"Oh, you're seeing Nick?" Kay grinned at her.

Meagan shook her head. "Not the way you are thinking. He asked me to help his little sister. Tori is a sweetie—and so excited about homecoming she made me wish I was in high school again. Just for a minute, though. I really wouldn't want to do it all over again!"

"I wouldn't want to go back, either, but I know what you mean. Homecoming is different. Denny and I will be going. My little brother is on Bay High's team. He's the quarterback."

"Oh, that would make it really fun, to have someone to cheer for."

"Why don't you go with us?"

"I might just take you up on that, if Denny wouldn't mind."

"He'd be glad to have you."

Kay's expression became dreamy, prompting Meagan to ask, "How is Denny doing?"

Kay's smile lit up her face. "He's fine, better than fine, really. He'll soon be my husband."

It took a minute for Meagan to realize what Kay was saying. "You mean he finally popped the question?"

Kay laughed and nodded. "He did."

Meagan jumped up to give her a hug. "I am so happy for you! Have you set a date yet?"

"No, but we are having an announcement party in a few weeks. I'll call you with a date as soon as I have it firmed up. I want you to be sure to be there. In fact, I'd like to ask you now, if you'll be my maid of honor."

"I'd be glad to." Meagan smiled. She truly was so happy for Kay; she'd been in love with Denny for a long time. "Will it be a winter wedding, do you think? Or are you wanting to be a June bride?"

"Truthfully, I've waited long enough. It doesn't matter what month, but the sooner, the better as far as I'm concerned!"

"Well, let me know what you need me to do, okay? Have you told anyone else? Or is it going to be a secret until you announce it at your party?"

"I'm thinking I'd like to keep it a secret," Kay said.

"Then I'll keep my mouth shut."

"Thanks, Meagan."

Meagan's break lasted longer than usual as they discussed wedding plans, and when she went back down to the shop, it was almost closing time.

She really was thrilled for Kay and Denny, but Kay's excitement made Meagan realize that she didn't have that same feeling when she thought of her and Thad's wedding. Not wanting to follow the direction her thoughts were leading her, she shook them off as she closed up shop and went back upstairs. While she showered and changed into something comfy, she found herself looking forward to dinner with Hattie and Tori Chambers later in the week. Meagan couldn't help wondering if she'd done the right thing by accepting Hattie's invitation—it was Nick's family after all. But, as confused as she was about her feelings for him, she really liked his sister and grandmother and looked forward to their company.

She checked her answering machine, just to make sure Nick hadn't left another message, but all that was there was the one she'd left there from the night before. She played it again and then, feeling silly, she deleted it. She wasn't a teenager like Tori. She was an adult, and she couldn't afford to let herself get caught up in teenage dreams all over again.

Yet, she couldn't help thinking how nice it would be to go to homecoming, especially if Nick asked her to go.

Argh! Disgusted with herself, she went to the kitchen to make a grilled cheese. She had to quit thinking of the man!

nine

With all her family out of town and none of her friends available, Meagan had to admit she was a little lonely the next night. She and her mother tried to touch base with each other most nights by talking to each other around ten o'clock, but tonight the phone was unusually quiet.

She flipped channels trying to find something that interested her, but her mind kept wandering. She was thrilled with the way Meagan's Color Cottage had taken off, and she was pleased with her employees. She no longer felt the need to check on them every little minute, and soon there wouldn't be a need for her to work long days anymore.

She'd be able to spend a little more time with her family, and she would be able to visit friends and have them over—at least until she went back to Dallas. Only trouble was, all her friends were married or, like Kay, had a significant other in their lives. Meagan sighed. She wanted the same things: a husband and a family of her own. And she could have all that with Thad. But she was uncertain about her future with him—or even if her future was with *him*. She wasn't even sure she wanted to go back to Dallas. She loved being back in Magnolia Bay. And after all, she *could* set up her offices anywhere she wanted.

More confused than she'd ever been in her life and so into her thoughts was she that when the phone rang a little after ten, Meagan jumped and nearly spilled the cup of tea she was bringing to her mouth.

She set it down carefully before lifting the receiver. "Hello?"

"Hi, Meagan. I hope I'm not calling too late."

Her heart gave a funny little twist at the sound of Nick's voice. "No. I've been watching television." *Or trying to, anyway.*

"I just got back from dinner with a client, and I checked in with Grams. She said you helped Tori pick out a beautiful outfit."

"It is." She couldn't resist teasing him. "Tori charged your card to the limit."

"Oh, she did, did she?" Nick chuckled.

"Nah. She actually looked at a few things and decided they were too expensive. She's going to look lovely, though."

"Not too lovely, I hope."

Meagan shook her head at the tone in his voice. He truly wasn't thrilled about this stage of his sister's life. "Oh, Nick. Tori is going to be fine! She seems to have a really level head."

"I hope so. I've been going back and forth over this homecoming thing. I hope I'm doing the right thing by letting her go."

"You know she would have resented it if you'd told her no."

"I know." He sighed. "I just wish she wasn't growing up so fast. It's that life goes on as usual, and then one day you wake up and suddenly your baby sister is no longer a baby. I don't like it one bit."

Meagan had to laugh. "I know. But you can't stop it from happening, Nick."

"I know I can't. Thank you for letting me complain about it. And thank you for helping her to pick something she likes."

"You're welcome. And your grandmother has already

thanked me. In fact, she asked me to dinner tomorrow night."

"She said she did. I told her she could have waited until I got back."

Meagan's heart skittered at the tone in Nick's voice. It sounded like he really would have liked to be there. "She said she and Tori were lonesome when you aren't there for supper."

"Aha. She made you feel sorry for them."

"She didn't have to do that. I like them both a lot, and I'm looking forward to it."

"So are they, Meagan. Thank you for accepting."

She didn't know quite what to say next and was glad she didn't have to when Nick continued, "Tori's excitement about homecoming is catching. It almost makes me wish I were back in school."

"I know. I was thinking the very same thing today when she came in." Meagan didn't add that she'd daydreamed about Nick asking her to go.

"I'm debating on going. After all it *is* homecoming, and alumni are expected to show up. We're supposed to be there. And. . .I could also keep an eye on Tori."

Meagan chuckled. "Now the truth comes out."

"Well, it's a thought." Nick laughed before he changed the subject. "How did your day go?"

Meagan smiled. She did love him asking about her day. "Fine. Kay came in late, and I took a break with her. How was yours?"

"Good. I have several appointments set for tomorrow, but I should be home the next day. How are things with Kay and Denny? I keep expecting to hear an engagement announcement anytime."

Meagan wondered if he'd been talking to Denny, and she had to stop herself from sharing Kay's news. "Kay says they're doing real well. She said something about having a get-together soon."

"Maybe they'll announce something then."

"That would be nice." Meagan had the feeling he was trying to get her to tell him something he already knew, and she hurriedly changed the subject before she let the cat out of the bag, just in case he didn't know.

"Wonder if they are going to the homecoming game," Nick said, seemingly out of the blue.

"Oh, yes. Kay said they are. Her brother is on the team."

"That's right, he is," Nick said. "Maybe we should get a group together. What do you think?"

"That sounds like fun." She didn't tell him she might be going with Kay and Denny.

"Will you go with me?"

Meagan's heart nearly did a nosedive into her stomach. "I'd like that."

"Great. I'll try to get a group together. We have a few weeks, don't we?"

"It's two weeks from this Friday."

"Okay. I'm looking forward to it!"

Meagan laughed. "You're just glad you found a way to spy on Tori."

"No." Nick's voice seemed deeper than usual. He cleared his throat, but it didn't seem to help as he continued, "I'm looking forward to spending time with you, Meagan."

Meagan knew he was getting under her skin. She was caring too much about this man. Maybe she should back out of the date. No, she couldn't bring herself to do that. She just plain didn't want to. "It'll be fun."

"Well, I've kept you up long enough. You have a nice time at my house tomorrow night."

"Thanks. I'm sure I will." Meagan found herself wishing he'd be there, too.

"I'll see you soon. I find myself missing you, Meagan."

Her heart flooded with joy at his words. "I. . ." She wanted so badly to say the words she couldn't say to Thad. Still she held them back now.

"Night, Meagan."

"Good night, Nick," she said softly. She heard the click on his end, but she held the receiver close to her heart for a moment before hanging it up. She could no longer deny that her feelings were growing for Nick Chambers. But it was Thad who was waiting for an answer to a proposal. She did need to see him. When he came to see her everything would be all right. By then, she'd know for sure what to tell him. Surely she would.

❧

Meagan was a little nervous when she got to Nick's the next evening, but Hattie and Tori put her at ease immediately.

"Come on in the kitchen, Meagan. Grams nearly has supper all ready," Tori said, leading her through the spacious living room and into the kitchen.

"Meagan, welcome to our home," Mrs. Chambers said as she popped a pan of biscuits into the oven beside a casserole dish.

"Thank you, Mrs. Chambers. It was very nice of you to invite me."

"We've wanted to ask you over for a while now," the older woman said. She motioned to the table that had already been set. "Just sit down and make yourself comfortable. And please, dear, 'Mrs. Chambers' is too formal."

"Isn't there something I can do to help, Miss Hattie?"

"Not a thing. Just keep me company, dear."

The aroma in the kitchen had Meagan's mouth watering. "Whatever you are cooking smells wonderful."

"It sure does," a voice behind her said. She whirled around to see Nick standing in the doorway. "And, if I'm not mistaken, I think it's my favorite: chicken and rice casserole." He smiled at Meagan from across the room.

"Nicky! You're home early," Tori said. "I'll set another place at the table! You're right; it is your favorite. We asked Meagan over to thank her for all the help she's given me."

"So I see." Nick winked at Meagan before crossing the room to kiss his grandmother on the cheek. "Actually, I knew she'd be here. And since my last appointment was canceled, I decided to come on home so I could have supper with you all."

Meagan's heart did a double flip and seemed to land somewhere near her stomach at the grin Nick flashed her as he loosened his tie and rolled up his shirtsleeves. After washing his hands, he took the casserole dish Hattie removed from the oven and brought it to the table.

Hattie and Tori followed with the biscuits and a salad.

"Nick, would you please say grace?" Hattie asked.

Nick reached for her hand and Tori took the other as they made a circle and he said a prayer before their meal.

Meagan's heart warmed at his words, and she was surprised at how right it felt to be sharing a meal with him and his family. Tori entertained them with stories from school, and Hattie promised to give Meagan the recipe for the wonderful casserole.

Dessert was a luscious butternut pound cake served with ice cream, and by the time they finished it, Meagan was so full she couldn't imagine being hungry for days. She insisted on helping to clean up the kitchen and that became a family affair, too. Or at least it started out that way. Then, Tori got a phone call and ran upstairs to take it in her room, leaving Nick to dry dishes while Meagan washed. Hattie finished clearing the table and went to her kitchen desk in the corner of the room to copy the recipe Meagan had requested.

Nick seemed to go out of his way to make her feel relaxed, which she did—maybe a little too much so. Sharing the simple chore of doing dishes with him gave her a warm feeling. It felt so comfortable being with Nick and his family, Meagan dreaded going back to her empty apartment. And that was exactly why she didn't stay for the movie Tori and Nick tried to get her to watch with them when the teenager came back downstairs. Being here felt *too* comfortable. She had to protect her heart. She couldn't afford to lose it to Nick again. She just couldn't.

❧

Nick walked Meagan to the car, wishing she would stay longer. He hated to see her go. It felt so right having her in his home, in his kitchen, beside him at the sink.

He opened the door for her but put a hand to her shoulder before she slid into the seat. "I'm glad I was able to come home early. Thank you for accepting Grams's invitation. We all enjoyed your company."

"I enjoyed it, too," Meagan said. Her gaze met his, and Nick wanted nothing more at that moment than to kiss her good night, but she slipped into the car and started it up before he could act.

Still, he couldn't let her get away without making sure he'd see her again. "I talked to Jeff about homecoming. He said he'd like to go and that maybe he'd ask Ronni to go with him—only as friends, of course—if one of the other girls can handle the shop for you."

Meagan chuckled. "I think that can be arranged if she says yes."

Nick's heart soared. She was still planning on going with him. "How about we all go to dinner before the game?"

"That would be nice."

"I'll talk to Jeff about it tomorrow." Meagan nodded as she looked up at him. It was all he could do to not duck his head into the car and kiss her good night.

"I, uh, I guess I'd better be going. Please thank your grandmother again for me. It was a wonderful meal."

Nick had no choice but to let her go and, hard as it was, he took a step away from the car. "Will do. You be careful going home."

"I will." She put the car in gear and waved as she took off.

Nick watched the taillights of Meagan's car disappear down the street before turning to go back inside. She seemed almost in a hurry to leave; yet she'd appeared to enjoy herself while they were having supper, although she'd been a little quiet while they were doing dishes. Maybe it was because he'd come home unexpectedly.

He chuckled and shook his head as he headed back inside. Why did he always look for problems where Meagan was concerned? She'd agreed to go to homecoming with him. He needed to be content with that for the moment.

෪

On the drive home, and all day the next day, Meagan felt like she was on a roller coaster. One minute she was excited about going to homecoming with Nick, and the next she found herself wondering if she'd lost her senses. Why had she agreed to go to homecoming with him? *Because I want to.* And why had she accepted his grandmother's invitation to dinner? Why couldn't she just say no? *Because I didn't want to. I wanted to go.*

She'd enjoyed the evening at Nick's. It felt like home. *And. . .I wanted Nick to kiss me.* Just for a moment, she'd thought he might. She knew she should be glad he didn't; instead she was disappointed and angry with herself that she wasn't. Meagan hadn't been this confused even as a teenager.

She didn't even check her answering machine when she came in the door. She didn't want to know if Thad had called. She felt bad enough as it was—thinking about another man when Thad thought she was going to marry him. Instead she showered and got ready for bed. With the lights out and moonlight streaming in from the balcony, Meagan was drawn outside.

Looking up into the starry sky, she prayed silently. *Dear Lord, please calm my emotions and give me guidance in what You would have me do. I've never felt so mixed up in my life. I care about Thad. I know he is a wonderful Christian man and would make a wonderful husband. But I think he deserves more than a woman who is fighting feelings for her first love—more than a woman whose pulse races at another man's smile. Is it just because I'm away from Thad's gentle caring that I'm drawn to Nick? And has Nick really changed as he appears to have?*

Lord, please help me to sort my feelings for these two men out. In Jesus' name, amen.

ten

Meagan felt better the next week. She had put her trust in the Lord, and she knew He would answer her prayers.

Ronni had agreed to go to homecoming with Jeff—only as good friends, of course—and excitement about the big game was rising all over town. Several more of Tori's friends came in shopping for homecoming outfits and asking Meagan's advice on how they should do their hair, while even more women came in to find something to wear to the game. Magnolia Bay might be small, but loyalty to its high school was huge.

She and Thad had been playing phone tag most of the week, and Meagan wondered if that was the Lord's way of giving her time to come to some decision as to what to say to him. Was she going to accept his proposal or not?

In the meantime, she was going to put off making any decision until after homecoming, telling herself that she didn't need to feel bad. She was going with Nick as just friends, and they would be surrounded by other friends. They were going to cheer on Kay's brother and keep an eye on Tori at the same time.

On the Tuesday of homecoming week, the festivities were threatened when forecasters announced they were watching a tropical depression out over the Gulf of Mexico. Everyone watched the weather forecasts and prayed. On Wednesday it looked like it would miss them, but it wasn't until Thursday, when the system failed to develop into a severe storm, that one could almost hear a collective sigh of relief in Magnolia Bay and across the Gulf Coast. The game was on.

The cool front that had kept the system out to the west reached southern Mississippi just in time to make it a comfortable sixty-five degrees at game time on the early October day. Kay, Ronni, and Meagan had decided to go for kind of casual dressy comfort by choosing jeans and pairing them with nice hand-knitted sweaters in the school colors of blue-green and gold.

Meagan had decided not to have Meagan's Color Cottage stay open late so that any of her employees who wanted to could go to homecoming, but Sara volunteered to keep it open because she wasn't planning on going. As Meagan left everything in her hands and went upstairs to get ready, she felt almost like a teenager again.

Even though she'd been telling herself that it was only a gathering of friends, when Nick came to pick her up, she realized she hadn't been completely truthful with herself. It felt like a date to Meagan. He looked very handsome in his jeans and a gold and blue-green striped shirt.

"You look wonderful," he said as Meagan gathered her purse and they headed downstairs to his car. "Don't laugh, but I think I've been looking forward to going to this game almost as much as Tori has."

"So have I. Did her date pick her up on time?" They'd all decided to go to Mike's for dinner after the game, once Nick realized he didn't want to leave the house until Tori's date showed up. Meagan had wholeheartedly agreed with the decision.

"He did. He was a little early, in fact."

"Oh, I bet that made Tori even more nervous."

"I don't know about her, but I think my quizzing him as to their plans made him a little tense." Nick chuckled. "There for a minute or two, I even felt sorry for the guy."

Nick opened the door for Meagan, and she chuckled as she took her seat. "Did his answers satisfy you?"

Nick waited until he slipped into the driver's seat to answer. "For the most part. They are double-dating with his older brother, who was driving. I met him, too. They picked up Tori first and then the brother's date. Rod assured me they would have her home on time."

"That's good."

"I didn't tell him I'd be watching them like a hawk." Nick glanced over at her with a grin. "I think he might have guessed that I would when I told him I was going to be at the game."

Meagan couldn't help giggling. She thought it might be a lot more fun going to homecoming as an adult than as a young couple on their first date.

By the time they arrived at the stadium, Kay and Denny and Jeff and Ronni had claimed a whole row of bleachers for them. Even Debbie and Eric were there. As Meagan climbed up the steps to the seats midway up, Nick guided her up with a protective hand at her back, making her feel special.

"It's about time you two got here. We've already spotted Tori and her date for you," Jeff said as they moved down the row and took their seats beside him and Ronni.

"Oh?" Nick said, looking around. "Where are they?"

"To your right in the next set of bleachers, and down about three rows," Denny said from the other side of Jeff.

Meagan had to smile as she watched Nick try to find his sister without letting her know he saw her.

"I see her. Thanks, guys."

"She looks so grown-up, Nick," Kay said. "I didn't realize she was sixteen now."

"I know. I still can't believe she's that old. But it doesn't mean she's grown-up yet," Nick said. "It just means I'm not getting any younger."

"None of us are," Denny said.

"Well, I feel like a teenager tonight," Kay said, waving at Alice and Mike, who were on their way up the steps to join them all. "Here we are, the old gang, at a high school football game, just like old times."

Except it really isn't, Meagan thought. She'd never gone to a ball game with Nick; she'd only dreamed about it. And now, her dream had come true.

"Oh, this is going to be fun," Alice said as she and Mike sat down beside Meagan.

"You left your business on a busy night like this, Mike?" Jeff asked.

"Just until we all get back there. I have good employees and a great assistant manager. Besides, it appears that half the town is here." Mike grinned and pulled his cell phone out of his pocket. "Just to be on the safe side, and in case of an emergency, I have this with me."

"Smart man," Nick said.

The game got under way and between watching it and Tori and her date, there was never a dull moment. It was fun to sit there with some of her best friends and cheer the home team on. Kay's little brother was a great quarterback, and at halftime, his team was only two points down from one of the best teams in the state.

The men went for refreshments while the women promised to watch out for Tori without being too obvious.

Her date did seem very attentive, and she looked like she was having a wonderful time. Meagan hoped that she was.

When Kay mentioned that she wanted to have a get-together soon, she made no mention of her engagement, and Meagan could only surmise that she hadn't told the other women. She certainly wasn't going to bring it up. That was for Kay to do.

"Hey, we decided getting together was so much fun, we need to do it more often," Denny said as he led the other men back to their bleachers. "I think we should have a cookout at my place tomorrow evening. How does that sound?"

"Sounds great to me," Kay said, patting him on the shoulder as he took his seat beside her.

Watching the look that passed between the two, Meagan had a feeling they would announce their engagement then. "Me, too," she added.

"We're furnishing the steaks, potatoes, and salad," Denny said.

"Well, who could turn that down?" Nick asked.

"How about you girls furnishing the desserts?" Jeff asked.

"I can make a cake," Meagan said. "I have a great recipe for a chewy chocolate cake."

"Mmm, sounds wonderful," Ronni said. "I'll bring ice cream."

"Great. Let's aim for around seven thirty," Denny said. "Kay and I will furnish everything else."

Meagan found herself looking forward to the next night almost as much as she'd looked forward to this one.

"Do any of you know that man?" Ronni asked, nodding her head in the direction of the bleacher steps. "He seems to be trying to get our attention."

Meagan's stomach sank when she turned to look; it was Thad. He smiled and waved. She waved back. As he made his way up the steps, she went to meet him, very much aware that her dream was quickly turning into a nightmare of her own making.

Thad gave her a quick hug as soon as he reached her. "I couldn't wait any longer. I had to see you. We've been playing phone tag too much lately."

"How did you know where to find me?" She didn't know what else to say, and she could feel at least seven pairs of eyes on her every move.

"I stopped by the shop and your employee told me where you were. She gave me directions on how to find the stadium, but I think I could have found it on my own from all the cheering I've heard. Sounds like a good game."

Meagan wasn't sure if she should ask him to join her group or find another place to sit, but it was Nick who came to her aid by motioning them on into the row of bleachers. Mike and Alice had moved down so that Meagan and Thad could sit on the end. Still at a loss for words, Meagan didn't know what to say, so once again Nick filled the gap by introducing himself and the others to Thad. Meagan had no doubt that each of her friends was very curious, but they showed their true loyalty to her by not asking any embarrassing questions. For that she was extremely thankful.

The second half began, and everyone's attention turned back to the game. Meagan had never felt more uncomfortable in her life as she sat a person away from the man who brought her, holding hands with the man who was waiting for an answer to his proposal. How would she go about saying she was sorry to both of them?

❧

Nick stewed in silence. So this was the man Meagan had been dating in Dallas. The night had been going really well from his point of view until this Thad person had shown up. He was pretty sure that Meagan hadn't known the man was coming. She seemed quite surprised to see him. And he seemed quite thrilled to see her.

Nick certainly couldn't blame him for coming to see her. He wouldn't have been able to stay away from Meagan, either, if he were in the other man's position. And Nick would like nothing better than to send the man from Texas right back where he came from.

It was almost impossible to pay attention to the game. When he wasn't watching Tori and her date, he was trying *not* to glance over at Meagan and Thad. When the game ended with Bay High the winner, cheers went up all over the stadium, and Nick felt like a fifth wheel as the couples around him hugged each other. Were it not for Thad's appearance, he'd be hugging Meagan right now.

Mike suggested that they all go back to the Seaside Surf and Turf for a late supper, including Thad, and Nick didn't know whether to be pleased or angry when Thad accepted for himself and Meagan. On one hand Nick didn't want to spend the rest of the evening watching them together, but neither did he want to think of them being alone for all that time.

When Tori and her date suddenly appeared beside him with several other young couples to ask if she could go to an after the game party at one of her friend's homes, he was almost grateful for the interruption to his thoughts and the conversations going on around him.

"Please, Nicky. I promise to be home on time," Tori pled.

"She will be, Mr. Chambers. You have my word," Rod added.

While Nick didn't know her date well enough to trust his word yet, he did know the Mayfields, the parents of the friend who was hosting the party, and he was sure she would be fine. In fact, they were on the sidelines waiting for the group of young people. Nick saw them and waved. When the Mayfields waved back, he smiled at his little sister. "I guess you can. Just be sure to meet that curfew."

"Thank you!" Tori hugged him and waved at Meagan and the rest of his friends. If she was puzzled after seeing an unfamiliar man standing with his arm around Meagan, she didn't show it. She was probably too excited about the party she was going to, to pay it much attention.

Watching her run down the bleacher steps with the others to join the Mayfields, Nick was glad that at least Tori was having a wonderful time tonight. His night had steadily gone downhill.

As his group started down the steps, he felt a soft grip on his shoulder. When he turned it was to find Meagan right behind him, with Thad at her side. She seemed a little uncomfortable at the situation and that gave him a little comfort.

"Nick, Tori seems to be having a great time. Don't worry about her. She'll make that curfew."

She did seem a little flustered—as well she should to Nick's way of thinking. "Thanks. I'm sure she will. And I'm glad one of us. . ." Nick caught himself just in time. There was no point making Meagan feel bad. She clearly hadn't known Thad was going to show up. And besides, he *was* the man she'd been dating back in Dallas. She'd only agreed to try to be friends with Nick. She certainly didn't owe him any explanation.

She just stood there looking at him—and he finally noticed that the smile on her lips didn't quite reach her eyes.

"Come on, you guys!" Mike shouted from several steps up. "Let's get this show on the road. Alice is starving."

Everyone laughed at that, knowing full well it wasn't Alice, but her husband, who was hungry. Nick turned and led the way out to the sidelines.

❧

As the group made its way to the parking lot, Meagan couldn't remember when she'd ever been quite so miserable. Nick looked so confused, and Thad was way too quiet—and she didn't know what to say to either one of them.

"Your friends all seem very nice," Thad finally said as he opened the car door for her.

"They are. I've known them all for years—some of us went to grade school together."

Thad only nodded before going around to the driver's side of the luxury car. "It was nice of them to include me in the invitation to dinner."

"We don't have to go, if you'd rather not." Meagan wasn't sure she wanted to go—not with both Thad and Nick there.

"I don't mind—unless you want to skip it?"

"No. That's fine. I'm sure you are starving after that long drive. Mike's restaurant has excellent food."

"I am kind of hungry."

She nodded to the car in front of them. Mike and Alice were just pulling out of the parking lot. "Then just follow Mike; he'll get us there."

"Will do." Thad moved his car out into traffic.

She ignored the urge to look around and see if Nick was

coming, too. She wouldn't blame him if he didn't show up. After all, he'd had a date of sorts when the evening started. But knowing she was a little disappointed in the way the evening was turning out, she could be projecting her own feelings onto Nick. He might not be bothered at all.

Meagan was relieved when they arrived at the restaurant before she had time to think about why she was disappointed. She didn't want to think about all of that now. Mike had reserved a side room for their group and had a small buffet table set up. It didn't take long for them all to serve themselves and gather at the big round table in the center of the room. Nick took a seat between her and Alice while Thad and Mike sat on the other side of them. Meagan had never felt more stifled than she did at that moment. It was as if Nick was reclaiming her as his date, and Thad was claiming her as his bride to be. She tried to eat but ended up just pushing the food around on her plate.

She held her breath when talk turned to the cookout planned for the next night.

"Thad, consider yourself invited, too," Denny said.

Meagan could have throttled her old friend. He should have left it up to her to decide whether to let Thad know about the cookout.

"Why, thank you. Whatever Meg wants to do is fine with me."

Meg? What is he doing calling me Meg? He's never done that before. Meagan couldn't even find her voice.

"Well, you both must come," Kay said. "It's going to be a special night, and Meagan really needs to be there."

That got Meagan's attention and as she exchanged looks with Kay, she was pretty sure the other woman was letting her know that she and Denny planned to announce their engagement the next night. She had to go. "Guess we'd better go, then."

Thad nodded and grinned. "We'll be there."

Meagan braved a glance at Nick, but he was paying attention to something Jeff was saying to him. Instead she caught the sympathetic glance Ronni gave her and decided right then and there that she'd had enough of the evening.

Ronni turned to Jeff and said, "I think it's time I got home, if you don't mind. I'm kind of tired, and I want to check on Claudia. She hasn't been feeling too well lately."

Meagan could have hugged her. She was more than glad to be able to call an end to the evening, too.

"Yes, I think we'd better be going, too," she said. "That is if you are ready, Thad."

He stood immediately and pulled out her chair. "Any time you are, love."

By the time they arrived back at her apartment, Meagan wondered if Thad felt as uncomfortable as she did. Something had changed in their relationship; there was no denying it. But she didn't want to think about it just yet. He'd traveled a long way to get here, and she wanted him to enjoy the rest of his weekend. She suggested that they go to Hide-a-Way Lake and have lunch with her parents the next day.

"I'd like that," Thad said as they walked up the stairs to her door. "It will be good to see your parents again."

"They'll love seeing you, too." She unlocked her door and turned back to him, hoping he wouldn't ask for an answer to his proposal tonight.

He didn't. In fact, he surprised her by saying, "You look tired. And I've got some work to do on my laptop back at the motel. I'm going to let you get some sleep, and I'll see you in the morning."

Meagan nodded. There was only one motel in Magnolia Bay's city limits, and while it wasn't part of a big chain, it was clean and comfortable from what Meagan had heard. "I–it was nice of you to come with all that work you have to do, Thad. I hope this trip doesn't put you behind on anything."

Thad shook his head and smiled down at her. "It won't. I needed to come. We'll talk tomorrow, okay?" He gave her a sweet kiss on her forehead before heading back downstairs to his car.

Meagan gave him a wave as he reached his car and looked up at her. She watched him drive off and unexpected tears flooded her eyes at the realization that everything had changed tonight.

Slipping out onto the dark balcony, she took a deep breath and looked out into the starry night. Thinking back over the evening, she'd known she couldn't marry Thad the moment she saw him at the game. Instead of being thrilled to see him, she'd been almost irritated that he'd picked that moment to show up. She'd been having a wonderful time with Nick, and he'd interrupted it all. Now she felt horrible that she hadn't been happy to see Thad. How could she have let herself fall out of love with him? And when did it happen? He was a wonderful Christian man, and she'd loved him, hadn't she? Now she wondered if what she felt for him had ever been the kind of love he deserved from the woman he'd asked to marry him.

Suddenly Meagan knew it had never been that kind of love and that was why she hadn't been able to give him an answer right away. She did love him—as a wonderful friend and brother in Christ and even though she knew he would make someone a marvelous husband, he wouldn't be hers. Her heart just didn't beat faster in his presence; her pulse didn't race when he smiled at her—not like it did with Nick. And Thad deserved so much more than she could give him.

Tears ran down her cheeks, and her heart broke a little for Thad, as she finally admitted to herself that she couldn't marry him and would have to tell him so before he headed back to Dallas.

Dear Lord, please forgive me for leading Thad to believe that I might marry him. I did think I cared enough, but now I'm afraid I'm in danger of losing my heart to Nick once more. And I may well be in for heartbreak all over again. I know how that feels, and I hate that I might be the one to break Thad's. No matter what happens with me and Nick—it wouldn't be right to keep Thad hanging on until I know, because I don't love him in that way, and I have to find a way to tell him. Please give me the right words to say to Thad and the wisdom to know what to do about Nick. In Jesus' name, I pray. Amen.

eleven

By the time Kay and Denny's party rolled around the next evening, Meagan was a bundle of nerves. She felt she owed it to Thad to take off work while he was in town, and they'd spent most of the day at Hide-a-Way Lake at her parents' place. They'd all gone swimming and skied the morning away, then showered and changed before going to lunch at the lodge.

Thad hadn't brought up his proposal, and she was relieved. She knew she had to let him down; she just wasn't sure when or how to do it. All she knew was that it had to be done before he went back home.

Her parents had always been kind to her friends, and they welcomed Thad easily. They had always read her well, and she'd never been more appreciative of that fact than she was today. They seemed to realize something was amiss, and her dad and mother appeared to go out of their way to avoid talking about the two of them as a couple, instead asking Thad about his work and the new projects he was working on.

Of course Meagan realized that much as her parents would like to see her happily married, they would love for her to decide to stay in Magnolia Bay, closer to them instead of going back to Dallas. They'd already mentioned, more than once, that she could easily run her chain of shops from anywhere.

Just as she and Thad were about to leave for Magnolia

Bay, her dad suggested showing Thad the new fishing boat he'd just bought. She could have hugged him for it. And it didn't surprise her one bit when her mother pulled her aside as soon as they were out of earshot.

"Did he come for an answer to his proposal?" she asked.

"I think so." Meagan nodded. "But I don't think I can tell him yes, Mom."

Her mother hugged her. "I know, honey. I can tell. You've found that you don't really love him, haven't you?"

"Not enough." Meagan shook her head and sighed. "Certainly not the way he deserves." *And nothing like the way I feel about Nick.* "Oh, Mom, I feel so awful." She couldn't hold back the tears that formed at her admission.

Her mother patted her back. "I know you do. It's not easy to tell someone you can't marry them, especially when he probably thought you would say yes."

"And I let him think it, Mom. What kind of person am I?" Meagan grabbed a paper towel and dabbed at her eyes.

"Meagan, I think you thought you *did* love him when you left Dallas. But in this case, absence hasn't made the heart grow fonder. It will be hard to tell him, but he has to know. And it's much better that you face how you feel now, than to marry him without loving him the way you should."

"Oh, I know that, Mom. I just don't want to hurt him. And there is no way to keep from doing that."

"I know." Her mother gave her a nudge. "I think your dad and Thad are on their way back. Go wash your face and freshen up, or he'll know before you get a chance to say anything. Hard as it will be to tell him, I don't think you want him to find out right this minute. I'm sure you've been praying, dear. And I'll pray that the Lord will give you the right words to say, too."

"Thank you, Mom." Meagan hurried upstairs to disguise the evidence of recently shed tears as best she could.

On the way back to Magnolia Bay, she was relieved that Thad kept the conversation on her dad's new boat and how nice and peaceful it was at the lake. When he left her at the shop so that she could check on things and bake the cake she'd promised to take to the cookout, Meagan was more than a little thankful to have some time to herself. She had to find the words to tell him she couldn't marry him, and she had to do it by tonight.

⁂

Nick wondered if he was just a glutton for punishment as he parked his car and headed for Denny's backyard. Spotting Meagan and Thad across the lawn, he conceded that he must be. His chest tightened in pain just to see her with another man, and he realized he'd been on the way to believing he actually had a chance to win her back. For a moment he thought he might turn and go back home, until he realized Thad had seen him.

No way was he going to allow the man to think he'd run him off. He waved as he approached the couple who'd been joined by several others.

"Hi, Nick," Denny said. "Glad you could make it."

"I wouldn't miss it."

He shook Thad's extended hand. "Evening, Thad. How are you enjoying your visit to our town?"

"It's a nice place. Actually, I'd like to see more of it, but that will have to wait for another visit. We spent most of the day with Meagan's parents and that was really nice."

Nick couldn't help the pang of jealousy that stabbed right through him. He really liked Meagan's parents and would love to spend some time with them at their place, but he had yet to be invited. He guessed that was reserved for the special people in Meagan's life. She looked lovely as she turned from listening to something Jeff was saying to him.

"Hi, Nick." She smiled at him and asked, "Did Tori get home on time?"

He relaxed slightly. Tori was a safe subject. "She did."

"And she had a good time?"

"I think so. Rod must have, too—he's called her three times today."

Meagan chuckled and patted him on the back. "Uh-oh. That sounds kind of serious. Are you really ready for first love?"

You are my first love, and I think my only love. He shook the thought out of his head as he answered her. "No. I don't think so." Nick pulled his gaze away from her and looked up to see that Thad was watching the two of them closely.

"Those steaks smell really good." Meagan sniffed appreciatively.

About that time, Kay stuck her head out the patio door. "Meagan, are you going to help me with the salad?"

"Sure." Meagan turned to the men. "I guess I'd better go help Kay. You two behave."

Nick couldn't help wondering if she knew how badly he wanted to suggest that Thad Cameron go back to Texas—as soon as possible.

Even if Meagan didn't realize it, Nick had a feeling Thad did as they watched her walk off and he struck up a conversation.

"She's quite a lady," Thad said.

The man was getting no argument from Nick. "She is."

"I take it you've known each other a long time."

Nick nodded. "Yes, since she was around fifteen."

"I'm sure she was lovely even back then."

"She's always been beautiful—on the inside as well at the outside," he added.

"I proposed to her right before she left Dallas," Thad said, right out of the blue.

Inhaling a deep breath, Nick felt as if he'd just been kicked in the stomach. He wouldn't have been able to speak if he'd tried, and he was glad when Jeff walked up and started asking Thad about his work in advertising.

Nick didn't hear much of the conversation; all he could think about was the revelation that Meagan might be engaged to this man. Why hadn't she told him that fact when he'd asked about Thad that night at the restaurant when he'd called her? She certainly hadn't been acting like a woman about to accept a marriage proposal, or one who was already engaged.

Thad seemed to be a likable guy, but the only man Nick wanted Meagan to marry was *him*. He left the other two men talking as he headed over to watch Denny take steaks of the grill. It appeared his dreams of a future with Meagan had just been shattered.

It was the longest evening he'd ever spent. When Denny and Kay announced their engagement, his gaze met Meagan's as she sat beside Thad. Nick held his breath waiting for a second announcement to be made. When it wasn't forthcoming, he didn't know whether to be hopeful or miserable. Nick took a deep breath and sent up a silent prayer to be able to accept the Lord's will no matter what the outcome.

As Meagan and Thad left the party and started back to her apartment, she knew time was running out. She had to tell him she couldn't accept his proposal, but in complete contrast to the night before, Thad was talkative.

"You have some really good friends, Meagan."

"Yes, I do. It was a nice surprise that it feels just as natural to be around them now as it did back when we were all in high school."

"I imagine it was." He pulled into the empty parking lot at Meagan's Color Cottage and turned to her. "How about we take a walk along the beach? We need to talk."

"I—okay." They did need to talk, and it wasn't going to be an easy conversation to have. It might be easier to tell him along the shore than right outside her door.

Thad took hold of her hand as they walked across Bay Drive to the public boardwalk and down the steps to the beach. Moonlight glistened on the waves rolling onto the sand and sliding back out again into the bay. Meagan thought how romantic the walk would be if only—

"Meagan." Thad slowed his steps. "We need to talk about the marriage proposal I gave you before you left."

"Yes, we do." *But how do I tell you—*

"I'm not sure how to say this, but"—he stopped and turned her toward him, looking deep into her eyes—"I can't marry you."

Relief flooded through Meagan, and she sent up a silent prayer of thanks that she didn't have to tell him. Yet she was taken by surprise and wasn't quite sure what to say. "I, uh, is there someone else?"

"Not for me. But I've come to realize that there may be for you."

Nick.

"At the very least, I know that you don't love me in the way I love you."

He was right, and the relief Meagan had felt only moments before turned to remorse. She felt awful that she couldn't return his feelings. One of the hardest things she'd ever done was to look him in the eye. "Thad, I really thought that I did love you and I never—"

"Meagan, I know you didn't lead me on. You wouldn't do that. The spark just isn't there, is it?"

She shook her head. "No." Tears welled up and escaped as she looked at him. "I never meant to hurt you, Thad."

He pulled her into a hug. "I know that. And it's probably a good thing that you came home. It would have been much worse if you'd married me thinking you loved me, only to find out later that you were still in love with someone else. You ought to think about moving your home office to Magnolia Bay since—"

Meagan began shaking her head. "No. I—there isn't anything—"

"What about Nick Chambers? There seems to be something there."

"There was, once. We dated in high school, but then he broke up with me and—"

"You still care—"

"I'm not sure how I feel."

"Well, for what it's worth, I think the man is crazy about you."

Meagan tried to ignore the surge of joy she felt at his words. "What makes you think that?"

"I've been watching the two of you all weekend. I've seen the way he looks at you—and the way you look at him."

"But I—"

Thad touched a finger to her lips, stopping her protest. "Sweetie, you need to be honest with yourself. Your heart is here. I think you left it here a long time ago."

twelve

Meagan stood on her balcony and watched as Thad drove away. They'd said their good-byes at her door, and he'd be going back to Dallas the next day. He was such a special man. How could she not be in love with him? It was heart-wrenching to see him wave good-bye, knowing she'd hurt him. She certainly knew what it felt like to have a broken heart. Memories of her breakup with Nick resurfaced and for the first time she wondered if Nick had felt the way she did now.

From what Thad had said, it was obvious that he thought it was Nick who still held her heart. What good was that going to do her now? Yes, he seemed to have changed, but he'd hurt her in the past. Even if Nick did care now, as Thad thought he did, how could she trust him not to hurt her again? Pain from the past mixed with the pain from the present, and Meagan cried herself to sleep.

The next morning she felt the need to be with family and decided to meet her parents at their church. She wondered if Thad was on his way back to Texas. She felt horrible about hurting him and wanted to talk to her mother about it all. She had her chance when her dad announced he was going fishing with one of the neighbors after lunch.

He'd no more than shut the door when her mother proved how well she knew Meagan.

"You told Thad you couldn't marry him, didn't you?"

"No. He saved me from that. *He* told me he couldn't marry me!"

"Oh?"

Meagan had to chuckle at the tone in her mother's voice. Even though she'd recognized that Meagan didn't love Thad, she didn't sound pleased that he'd been the one to end the relationship. "Yes, Mom, that's what he said. And you know he was right. He knew I didn't love him enough. He seems to think I'm in love with someone else."

"And would he be right?"

"Oh, Mom. I think he may be. I do care for Nick—and he seems to have changed into the man I always imagined him to be."

"Well then—"

"But what if I'm wrong? I feel terrible about hurting Thad. I know how that feels. And I'm not sure I can take the chance of that happening again—with the same person. I just don't know if I can trust Nick any more now than I could back then."

"Honey, I've heard good things about Nick through the years. And I don't think you should judge him by the past, but by the man he's become."

Meagan shook her head. "I'm just not sure I can do that. And I'm not even sure about how he feels."

"Then pray about it and leave it in the Lord's hands. He'll make it all clear."

"I've been praying. But so far, I'm as confused as ever."

"Maybe you aren't truly leaving it all in *His* hands, dear. I'll pray that you do."

❧

Nick poured himself a cup of coffee and took a sip of the hot fragrant liquid, trying to get good and awake. He'd slept little, waking off and on and thinking back over the events of the night, until he'd finally decided to get out of bed. Had he lost Meagan? It certainly appeared that he was on the verge of doing just that—but then she'd never really been his to lose—not since high school. Still, he'd thought he was making progress in the last few weeks. And he felt as if the Lord had brought her home so that they could get back together. Could Nick have been totally wrong?

The ring of the telephone brought him out of his thoughts, but he was utterly unprepared to hear the voice on the other end.

"Nick? This is Thad Cameron. I hope I'm not calling too early for you."

Nick sent up a silent prayer that Meagan was all right. He could think of no other reason the man would be calling him, unless it was about her. "No, it's fine. I've been up for a while. What can I do for you, Thad?"

"I'm leaving for Dallas this afternoon, but I'd like to meet you for breakfast or lunch, if you are free."

Nick couldn't refuse. He had to find out what the man wanted to talk about. "I can do that."

"You name the place."

"The coffee shop down the street from Meagan's Color Cottage is a good place to eat. I can meet you for breakfast or lunch. What is best for you?"

"How about meeting for breakfast?"

Nick glanced at the kitchen clock. He'd have time. "I can be there in about thirty minutes."

"That's good. I'll see you there."

Nick hung up the phone and brought his cup to his mouth again. Obviously nothing was wrong with Meagan, or the man would have told him so. But what could he want to talk about if not her?

He hurriedly showered and changed before meeting up with his grandmother back downstairs. "I'll meet you and Tori at church, if that's all right with you, Grams. I'm meeting someone for breakfast."

If she was curious, she didn't voice it. "That's fine. We'll see you there."

Glad she wasn't asking for any explanations, Nick kissed her delicate cheek on his way out the door and promised, "I'll take you both to lunch, okay?"

It took only about ten minutes to get to the coffee shop, and Thad was waiting for him when he went inside. Nick didn't know whether to be relieved or disappointed that Meagan wasn't with him.

"Thanks for coming," Thad said, holding out his hand.

"No problem." They shook hands, and Nick slid into the booth across from him. Or at least Nick hoped there wasn't a problem. Before he could find out, the waitress showed up to take their orders.

"I'm glad you could meet me this early," Thad said once she'd left the table. "I'd like to get home in time to attend church tonight."

"You are driving?"

Thad nodded.

"It's a long trip."

The waitress brought Nick a cup of coffee and gave Thad a refill before Nick could comment.

When she left, Thad went on, "I guess you are wondering what I want to talk about."

"You could say that. I'm assuming it has to do with Meagan." *And praying she hasn't sent you to tell me you two are getting married.*

Thad took a sip from his cup before answering. "I think you should know. . ."

Nick's heart seemed to twist in his chest, and it took him a minute to register the rest of what the man was saying.

"Meagan and I have broken up."

Nick held his breath, and then let it out. "You've what?"

"Oh, it's not what I wanted—or hoped for when I came down—but this weekend it became obvious that we aren't meant to be together. She doesn't love me the way I love her."

Nick didn't know what to say. Inside he was rejoicing, but seeing the pain in the other man's eyes had him trying not to show the joy he was feeling.

"It's all right, Nick. I don't expect you to be sad for me."

Nick sighed and shook his head. Evidently he hadn't been successful in hiding his feelings. "I guess it's obvious that I'm not exactly disappointed by your news."

His respect for the man grew when Thad chuckled. "You could say that. You are in love with her, aren't you?"

Nick wasn't going to lie. "I am. I've been in love with her for years."

"Then what happened? She said the two of you broke up."

"We did. I was too young to handle what I felt for her back then," Nick said simply.

"I see."

Nick had a feeling that he did. "I'm not sure how she feels now."

"Does she know how you feel?"

"Not really. Maybe it's time I let her know."

"Maybe it is." Thad looked him straight in the eye. "If I were you, I'd do just that. In fact, I'd grab her quick. Because, as I'm sure you are well aware of, she's much too precious to let go of a second time."

The waitress showed up just then with their meal, interrupting their conversation.

When she left, Nick assured the other man, "I'll take your advice to heart, Thad."

"Good."

"You are a good man, Thad."

"And you'd better be, Nick."

For a fleeting moment Nick wished they weren't rivals. He had a feeling they could have been good friends.

❧

An inner happiness stayed with Nick for the rest of the day, but by the end of the week, he was beginning to think he'd never get a chance to tell Meagan how he felt. He'd called the shop repeatedly only to have Ronni tell him she was busy or unavailable.

When he tried her home, her answering machine didn't seem to be working. At least something wasn't working right because her line was always busy. He was about ready to go knock on her door and just ask her if she was trying to avoid him, but he didn't want to risk losing her friendship either. Maybe she was upset over the breakup with Thad. Maybe she had loved the man. Then he told himself that was a crazy thought. If she'd been in love with Thad, he would never have left without placing an engagement ring on her finger.

Nick had never felt more confused in his life. And yet, behind all the frustration of not knowing how she felt or what to do, there was still a flame of hope, now that he knew she and Thad weren't a couple. There was only one thing he could do at the moment. He prayed aloud.

"Dear Lord, please help me to know how to handle all of this. I truly believe that You brought Meagan back here for a reason. I pray it is for us to get back together. She doesn't seem to want to talk to me right now, and I'm not sure how much longer I can keep from going right over there and telling her how I feel. But I don't want to risk losing what ground I may have gained. Please guide me—and give me patience. In Jesus' name I pray, amen."

⋙

By the end of the weekend, Meagan was determined to distance herself from Nick and his family. She cared too much, and she was afraid that her feelings wouldn't be returned. After all, Nick had only asked that they try to be friends again—not that they fall in love. And much as it hurt to lose him all those years ago, it would be much worse now. There was no way she could be sure he wouldn't hurt her once more, and she just didn't think she could go through that pain all over again. Besides, after all she'd put Thad through, letting him think she might marry him, she just couldn't see how she deserved to have her heart's desire come true.

Somehow, she'd been fortunate in truly being busy with a customer or out when he called the shop. She certainly didn't want to have her employees lie for her. At home, she'd bought a laptop and began keeping it online so that her phone would only ring busy and she wouldn't have to hear his voice on the answering machine. She knew she wouldn't be able to resist picking up or returning his call if she heard his voice. No, she wouldn't be able to do that at all.

thirteen

By the middle of the next week, Nick was about to give up on contacting Meagan by telephone. She obviously didn't want to talk to him. He prayed for more patience, knowing that the Lord was in control and if it was in His plans for Meagan and him to get back together, it would happen, but only in His time.

When Tori came home from school crying the next week, necessity caused him to dial Meagan's home number one more time. He didn't have a clue how to deal with a brokenhearted teenage girl, and Meagan was the only one he trusted enough to ask for advice.

Much as he wanted to talk to her, he wished it hadn't been about his hurting sister. Seeing her cry broke his heart. She wouldn't talk to him or their grandmother about it, and he could only hope that Meagan would be able to help.

≥∙

Meagan realized that distancing herself from Nick and his family was easier said than done. For one thing, she had a message that Tori had called her at work, and she was debating whether to call her back or not. The other was that her mother wasn't happy that she had to call Meagan's cell phone just to get hold of her at night. Only minutes after she got offline to please her mother, the phone rang. She let the answering machine pick up and felt like a whole field of butterflies were let loose in her stomach when she heard Nick's voice on the other end.

It was his message that made her realize that she wasn't going to be able to stay away from him or his family.

"Meagan. I've been trying to call you for days. I hope everything is all right with you. I—look, I really would like to talk to you about so many things, but right now I need to talk to you about Tori. She and Rod evidently broke up, and she's done nothing but cry since she got home from school. I just don't know what to—"

Meagan grabbed the receiver. "Nick, I'm so sorry. Do you know what happened?"

She heard a huge sigh before he answered, "No, not really. Thank you for picking up. I really need some advice, Meagan."

She felt horrible for not returning his calls at work—and for not calling Tori this evening. *Dear Lord, what am I turning into? I seem to be hurting everyone I care about! Please help me.*

"Oh, Nick. She called the shop earlier today and I—what can I do?"

"Well, she's not really talking to me or Grams about it. I think maybe she would open up with you. Do you think you could call her and see if that's what she wanted?"

"I'd be glad to. When we hang up I'll call her."

Relief was evident in his voice. "Thank you, Meagan. I just don't know what to do, but my heart breaks every time I see her burst into tears, and I want to send that young man to another planet."

"You don't have any idea what happened?"

"No. She just said they broke up. When we ask anything more, she starts crying all over again and runs to her room."

"Okay. I'll call right back and see if she will talk to me."

"She's still up. I'll be sure to let her answer the phone

when you call. It shouldn't be a problem, though. She's been quick to grab it. I think she's hoping it's Rod."

"Probably so." Meagan could remember that feeling really well.

They said their good-byes, and Meagan waited a couple of minutes before dialing his number. The phone only rang once when Tori answered.

"Hello?"

Meagan had a feeling Nick was right in assuming Tori was hoping Rod would call. She hated to disappoint her.

"Tori, it's Meagan. I'm sorry I'm just now returning your call. What's up?"

"Oh, Meagan. I—"

Meagan could tell she was trying to hold back tears. "What's wrong, honey?"

"Rod and I broke up—and I needed to talk to you."

"Do you want me to come over now?"

"No, it's getting late, and I don't want to explain everything to Grams and Nicky right now. Could we talk tomorrow? I sure could use your advice."

"Of course. I can come over when you get out of school. What time?"

"I'll be home by four and that would be a good time. Grams is getting her hair done then, and Nicky won't be home from work yet. Are you sure you don't mind?"

"I don't mind at all, Tori. I'll be there at four."

"Thank you, Meagan." She sniffed.

Meagan's heart broke for her. "You're welcome. I'll see you tomorrow."

❧

By the time Meagan arrived at the Chambers' home the next afternoon, she wondered if she should just stay out of things. Yet, Nick had asked her to help, and she knew he was upset by not being able to help Tori.

His concern for his sister, along with all she'd observed about him since she'd been back—and what she'd heard from her friends—had her acknowledging to herself that he was a changed man. He'd grown into a wonderful Christian who took his responsibilities very seriously and who could love with all his heart. She had been guilty of misjudging him, and using the past to do so.

She rang the doorbell and was a little surprised when Nick's grandmother opened the door. "Meagan, dear, how nice to see you! Tori said you were coming by."

"I hope that's all right."

"Oh yes, dear. I'm just on my way out, but she's up in her room." Her voice lowered to a whisper. "I hope you can get her to talk to you. Nick said you would try."

"I'm going to do my best," Meagan whispered back.

Hattie patted her on the back. "Thank you." In a louder voice, she called, "Tori, Meagan is here!"

"Ask her to come on up, Grams, will you?" the young girl shouted down.

"You should feel honored," Hattie whispered once more. "She doesn't let just anyone in her room, and she's been straightening it ever since she got home. It's the first room to your right."

"I'll find it," Meagan said.

But she didn't have to. Tori met her at the top of the stairs and led her back to her room. It was a lovely, teenage girl's room, decorated in the colors Tori liked best, with pennants and pictures pinned up on a cushioned and covered bulletin board. There was a dressing table in one corner and a computer desk in another. An easy chair sat next to a table beside the bed.

"Please sit down, Meagan." She sat on the side of the bed, leaving the easy chair for Meagan. "Thank you for coming."

On the surface Tori seemed fine, but Meagan could see telltale signs of recent tears. Her mascara was a little smudged and there were used tissues on her dressing table.

Meagan sat down. "I'm glad to be here. Want to tell me what happened with you and Rod?"

The young girl's eyes filled with tears, and she dabbed them with a tissue. Meagan almost wished she hadn't brought up the boy's name, but she was here to help and he was the problem.

"Well, we broke up."

"Can you tell me why? Was he pressuring you about anything? He wasn't trying to get you to do anything against your will, was he?" Meagan sent up a silent prayer that wasn't the case. She'd been worried about that all day.

"No. Oh no, ma'am! It was nothing like that."

Relief flooded through Meagan at Tori's words. "Good. Then why did he break up with you?"

"He didn't break up. I did."

"Oh? I thought you liked him."

"I do—very much. But he wants me to see only him, and not even spend time with my friends. I told him I thought we were too young for that kind of commitment."

Meagan couldn't have been prouder of Tori if she'd been her own little sister. "He didn't like that so much, I guess."

Tori shook her head. "No. He didn't. He told me that if I couldn't go steady with him, we couldn't date at all. And I said I guess we couldn't date at all." She started to cry. "But, Meagan, I really care so much about him! I don't want to lose him!"

As she began to sob, Meagan sat down beside her and pulled her into her arms for a hug, rocking her back and forth. "Oh, honey, I'm so sorry you are hurting. But you did the right thing. You are awfully young to be going steady."

"You really think so?"

"I know so." Her assurance seemed to help and after a few minutes Tori's tears eased. Meagan went over to her dresser and pulled more tissues from the box and brought them back to her. "You know, Tori, I believe that if it is meant to be, you and Rod will get together again when the time is right."

"Do you?" Tori wiped her eyes and blew her nose.

Meagan leaned back against the dresser and tried to reassure her. "Yes, I really do."

"Is that what happened to you and Nicky?"

Taken by surprise, Meagan didn't know what to say. "What do you mean?"

"Grams said she thought you and Nicky really liked each other a lot when you were around my age. Did you?"

Meagan couldn't lie to the teenager. "Yes, we did. But we broke up."

"Why?"

Suddenly she remembered Nick telling her that he'd been too young to handle how he felt and that was why he'd stopped seeing her. Maybe he was wiser than she'd given him credit for all those years ago. She smiled at his little sister, thinking how much alike they were. "For very similar reasons to yours; we were too young."

"Well, you aren't that young now," Tori said with the bluntness of youth. "You are both back in the same town, and you've seen each other several times," Tori said. "Do you think it's God's will that you came back—so that you two could get together?"

Meagan didn't know. She wished that she did. Could it be? "I—"

"If it was meant to be, that would make sense, wouldn't it?" Tori wanted an answer, a positive one to give *her* hope.

"Honey, I just don't know. I guess maybe it is. I'm just not sure—" Meagan looked up to see Nick standing in the doorway looking at her. How long had he been there? And how much had he heard? Totally embarrassed, Meagan wasn't staying around to find out. Yet she couldn't just walk out on Tori. "I, uh, I need to be relieving Ronni at the shop. If you—are you all right, Tori?"

The young girl nodded and smiled at her. "Thank you for coming over. It helped a lot."

Meagan had a feeling Tori understood her need to run all too well. "If you need to talk. Anytime, night or day, just call me, okay?"

"Okay."

Nick hadn't moved, and she had to get out of that room. She felt more flustered by the minute.

"I'll talk to you soon, Tori."

With that she hurried past Nick and down the stairs, her heart pounding louder with each step she took. How much had he heard? And was Tori right? Were they meant to be together? Was that God's will all along?

❧

Nick had come home early hoping to run into Meagan. He hadn't been able to stay away. And he'd meant to let them know he was there, but when he got just outside Tori's room, he heard his name mentioned in their conversation, and he unabashedly listened in. As Tori kept pressing Meagan and he heard her answer, his heart began to sing with joy that maybe Meagan would finally realize what he had weeks ago—that God had brought them back together again for a purpose and that what they'd felt all those years ago was in His plans for the here and now.

But when he saw the look on her face when she spotted him just outside the door, he realized that she might only just be coming to that realization. As she flew past him and down the stairs, he decided that he might have to be patient awhile longer. He'd waited this long; with the Lord's help, he'd be able to wait a little longer.

fourteen

Meagan couldn't get away from the Chambers' home fast enough. She'd never been so flustered in all her life. Nick looked as if he'd been about to say something when she turned to run out of the room, but she was too embarrassed to stay and hear what it was. Now she could add cowardice to all of her other unflattering qualities.

If Ronni wondered why she rushed into the shop and began asking all kinds of questions about the next day's schedule, she didn't say anything and for that Meagan could have hugged her. She'd done enough talking today, and she had a lot to think about—but she didn't want to do it right now. Instead, she concentrated on placing orders and unpacking some new accessories that had come in that afternoon.

Before Ronni left for home, she asked, "Are you all right, Meagan? I mean—"

"I'm fine. Just a little muddled today."

"Well, if you need to talk or anything—"

"Thanks, Ronni. I might just take you up on that offer—if I ever sort things out enough to know where to begin."

"Just know you can call on me anytime, okay?"

"I do. And I appreciate it more than I can say. You have a good evening."

"You, too." Ronni headed for the door. "And don't work too hard."

"No, I won't," Meagan said. "Tell Claudia hello for me."

"Will do. See you tomorrow." Ronni waved and left for home.

Meagan went back to unpacking stock thinking about how blessed she was to have friends who cared. Both Kay and Alice had called to check on her during the week. Although she knew they were curious as to what was going on with her and Thad and Nick, they didn't ask too many questions. Alice invited her to the surprise shower/ engagement party she and Mike were throwing on Saturday of the next week, and Kay wanted her advice on colors for the wedding.

When she finally closed shop and went upstairs, it was to find two messages on her answering machine. One was from Tori, thanking Meagan for talking to her and telling her she felt much better. Meagan sent up a prayer of thanksgiving that she hadn't confused the young girl more by her sudden departure.

The other message was from Nick thanking her for taking the time to talk to Tori. "She seems better, Meagan. She even started supper before Grams got home. Once more, I owe you. Talk to you later."

She was relieved he hadn't called the shop and that she didn't have to talk to him just yet. But each time the telephone rang over the next few days, Meagan held her breath. On the one hand she wanted it to be Nick. On the other, she didn't know what she would say to him if it were. She seemed to be praying constantly about it all, but she was no closer to knowing how she felt or what she should do than the day she talked to Tori.

On Sunday she decided to go to church in Magnolia Bay instead of meeting her parents at their church. When she entered the church she'd grown up in, she was welcomed by old and new members alike, and it felt like coming home. The minister was new, but she'd heard he was very good and she looked forward to hearing his lesson. Taking a seat midway up on the right side, she smiled at those around her and looked to see if she recognized any others. When she spotted Nick, Hattie, and Tori several pews up, the joy she felt almost overwhelmed her.

Tears sprung to her eyes. All she'd heard about him finally sunk in. He *had* become a Christian. None of it had seemed real until this moment. All those years ago she'd tried to get Nick to go to church with her and her family, to no avail. At the time he wasn't going to church anywhere and didn't want to hear much about it. Still, even after they'd broken up, she'd hoped and prayed that he would become a Christian.

Now she could see clearly that he had become the man she wanted him to be: A wonderful Christian man, an even better man than she'd dreamed of—taking on all the responsibilities handed to him at an early age.

Meagan could no longer deny how she felt about Nick. She loved him. She had always loved him, and she was certain now that she always would. However, acknowledging that fact didn't mean that he loved her, or that she could let him know how she felt.

Meagan tried to concentrate on the service. The lesson came from Isaiah, and she felt sure the Lord was trying to get something across to her, but she didn't seem to be getting His message. When the service was over, she hurried out, waving only to several people. She didn't want Nick or his family to see her just yet—not until she could do a lot of soul-searching and understand what the Lord was trying to get her to see.

During that week, Meagan truly sought to grow closer to the Lord and to spend more time reading her Bible, hoping to find answers to what she should do about her relationship with Nick—if there even was one. She felt drawn to the book of Isaiah, and as she read from chapter forty-three, it finally dawned on her what it was the Lord was trying to get her to understand. She needed to quit dwelling on the past and forget the hurt from all those years ago. She loved Nick now, and she prayed he cared as much as she did. If they were ever to have a future together, she must choose to trust him with her heart and trust that the Lord would see them through. Without that trust there could be no future for them.

As the week wore on, she found herself wondering if Nick would be at the engagement party Mike and Alice were throwing for Denny and Kay. No one had mentioned him to her since Thad's visit.

As she got ready to go to the party, she found herself hoping Nick would be there yet nervous about how to act if he was. How did she let him know she still cared? Could she even risk letting him know until she found out how he felt about her?

Dear Lord, please let me know what to do. I think You may have brought me back here for more than just to open a much-needed new business in Magnolia Bay. I don't even know if Meagan's Color Cottage is going to be of any help in bringing this town more outside business, although I hope it does. But maybe the greater reason for me to come back was simply for Nick and me to get together again. I hope that is so, Lord. I love him. I pray he loves me, too. Please help me to find out. In Jesus' name I pray. Amen.

❧

It had been all Nick could do not to call or go by Meagan's the next week. He was trying to give her time and space to figure it all out. But as he dressed for Denny and Kay's engagement party, he made up his mind to let Meagan know how he felt tonight. If she didn't feel the same way, then he would have to deal with it and ask the Lord to help him accept it.

He had a good reason to approach her. Tori was doing much better this week, and he was sure Meagan had helped her. In fact, his little sister was feeling quite grown-up these days. She told him it was about time he attended to his personal life and that she was praying things would work out for him and Meagan.

As he arrived at the Seaside Surf and Turf, he found himself whispering the very same prayer. It took him only a minute to spot Meagan from the doorway of the room Mike had reserved for the party, and he wondered if he had inner radar where she was concerned. She was talking to Ronni and Alice, and when she looked his way, he felt as if his heart did a complete somersault before somehow settling back in his chest only to pound so hard and fast he could feel it in his ears.

The smile she gave him had his pulse racing as he crossed the room. Before he had a chance to say anything to her, Mike announced that Kay and Denny were on their way in. Nick settled for standing next to her quietly as everyone waited for the couple to clear the doorway of the room.

As soon as they did, a collective "Surprise" rang out over the room. Kay and Denny were welcomed amidst congratulations and laughter. With the attention firmly centered on the newly engaged couple, Nick took the opportunity grab Meagan's hand then led her toward the French doors leading outside. He'd waited long enough. He wasn't going to give her a chance to get away. "We need to talk."

"Nick! What is it? What's wrong? Is Tori all right?" Meagan asked.

"Tori is fine. I've wanted to thank you for talking to her. It helped more than you know. But it's not Tori I want to talk about."

"No? What then?"

"You—and me." Nick pulled her out onto the deck overlooking the bay and into his arms. He gazed into her luminous blue eyes and was encouraged by the expression in them. He lowered his head and his lips touched hers lightly at first. He was thrilled when she responded, and he deepened the kiss, filling it with all the love in his heart.

When their lips parted, he looked back down at her. "Did that tell you anything?"

"I think so…"

"Well, just in case the message got lost, I'll tell you what it said." Her smile gave him the courage he needed. "Meagan, I love you. I've loved you for all these years. I'd like to put the past behind us and spend the rest of our lives proving just how much I love you, if you will let me."

When Meagan stood on tiptoe to kiss him once more, he was pretty sure he had her answer. No words ever sounded sweeter to him than the ones she uttered as she broke the kiss. "I love you, too, Nick."

The Lord had answered his prayers, and he wasted no time. "Will you marry me?"

"Oh, yes, I will. I've finally realized that what I told Tori is true for us, too. If it's meant to be, it will happen, all in God's time."

epilogue

Meagan took a deep breath, and she and her dad waited for the wedding planner's signal to start down the aisle. Her long-ago dreams were finally coming true. It was a beautiful early December day, clear and cool, but not cold. Family and friends filled the church in Magnolia Bay. Nick's grandmother and Tori sat on the groom's side of the aisle while her mother sat on the other. Aunts and uncles, cousins and friends, filled the pews on both sides. This town she loved so much had turned out in force to see two of its own unite in marriage.

She hoped and prayed that Magnolia Bay would recover, that her business and the others beginning to spring up would be successful in helping the town grow again. In any case, she couldn't be happier to be starting her life as a married woman here in her hometown.

It was all sweeter than she'd ever imagined with Alice, newlywed Kay, and Ronni as her attendants, while Nick was joined by Denny, Jeff, and Mike. Their old group was now witnessing what they'd all been sure would happen those many years ago—the marriage of Nick Chambers and Meagan Evans.

She barely registered the gentle pressure of her dad's hand on hers, letting her know it was time to start down the aisle. As they began the slow measured walk, she caught her breath, her gaze held by the look in Nick's eyes as he watched her come down the aisle. He looked magnificent in his tuxedo, and his smile seemed only for her, drawing her ever closer, assuring her of his love.

As they recited their vows to love and to cherish all the days of their lives, her heart beat so hard she was sure Nick and everyone in the wedding party could hear it. They exchanged rings, and the minister pronounced them man and wife, adding, "You may now kiss your bride."

When Nick pulled her into his arms and kissed her, she found that his heart was beating every bit as fast as hers. "I love you," he whispered.

"I love you, too."

They turned toward the congregation as the minister introduced them. "I present to you Mr. and Mrs. Nick Chambers."

Nick pulled her hand through his arm, and they walked back down the aisle as a married couple. When they reached the reception area, Nick pulled her into his arms to kiss her once more, and she was overwhelmed by the joy she felt at being this man's wife. As his lips claimed hers, Meagan's heart was full of love and gratitude, and she sent a silent prayer upward, thanking the Lord above for bringing them back into each other's lives, assuring that the love she and Nick felt for each other always had been and would continue to be—simply unforgettable.

A Letter To Our Readers

Dear Reader:

In order that we might better contribute to your reading enjoyment, we would appreciate your taking a few minutes to respond to the following questions. We welcome your comments and read each form and letter we receive. When completed, please return to the following:

Fiction Editor
Heartsong Presents
PO Box 719
Uhrichsville, Ohio 44683

1. Did you enjoy reading *Unforgettable* by Janet Lee Barton?
   ❑ Very much! I would like to see more books by this author!
   ❑ Moderately. I would have enjoyed it more if

   _____

   _____

   _____

2. Are you a member of **Heartsong Presents**? ❑ Yes ❑ No
   If no, where did you purchase this book? _____

   _____

3. How would you rate, on a scale from 1 (poor) to 5 (superior), the cover design? _____

4. On a scale from 1 (poor) to 10 (superior), please rate the following elements.

   ____ Heroine   ____ Plot
   ____ Hero   ____ Inspirational theme
   ____ Setting   ____ Secondary characters

5. These characters were special because? _____

_____

_____

6. How has this book inspired your life? _____

_____

_____

7. What settings would you like to see covered in future
Heartsong Presents books? _____

_____

_____

8. What are some inspirational themes you would like to see
treated in future books? _____

_____

_____

9. Would you be interested in reading other **Heartsong
Presents** titles? ❏ Yes ❏ No

10. Please check your age range:

    ❏ Under 18   ❏ 18-24

    ❏ 25-34   ❏ 35-45

    ❏ 46-55   ❏ Over 55

Name _____

Occupation _____

Address _____

City, State, Zip _____

North Carolina

3 stories in 1

Unlikely romances unfold in North Carolina. Deidra Pierce seems to have it all—until Eli McKay and his daughter enter her life. Liza Stephens is rescued by a nice guy—then she discovers his real identity. Fun-loving mortician Sharley Montgomery is completely at home in the small town—until Kenan Montgomery rocks her world. Can forgiveness and love find a way?

Titles by author Terry Fowler include: *Carolina Pride*, *Look to the Heart*, and *A Sense of Belonging*.

Contemporary, paperback, 368 pages, 5³⁄₁₆" x 8"

———————————————————————

Please send me ____ copies of *North Carolina*. I am enclosing $6.97 for each. (Please add $2.00 to cover postage and handling per order. OH add 7% tax.)

Send check or money order, no cash or C.O.D.s, please.

Name_____

Address _____

City, State, Zip _____

To place a credit card order, call 1-740-922-7280.
Send to: Heartsong Presents Readers' Service, PO Box 721, Uhrichsville, OH 44683

Heartsong

CONTEMPORARY ROMANCE IS CHEAPER BY THE DOZEN!

Any 12 Heartsong Presents titles for only $27.00*

Buy any assortment of twelve *Heartsong Presents* titles and save 25% off the already discounted price of $2.97 each!

*plus $2.00 shipping and handling per order and sales tax where applicable.

HEARTSONG PRESENTS TITLES AVAILABLE NOW:

___HP421 *Looking for a Miracle*, W. E. Brunstetter
___HP422 *Condo Mania*, M. G. Chapman
___HP425 *Mustering Courage*, L. A. Coleman
___HP426 *To the Extreme*, T. Davis
___HP429 *Love Ahoy*, C. Coble
___HP430 *Good Things Come*, J. A. Ryan
___HP433 *A Few Flowers*, G. Sattler
___HP434 *Family Circle*, J. L. Barton
___HP438 *Out in the Real World*, K. Paul
___HP441 *Cassidy's Charm*, D. Mills
___HP442 *Vision of Hope*, M. H. Flinkman
___HP445 *McMillian's Matchmakers*, G. Sattler
___HP449 *An Ostrich a Day*, N. J. Farrier
___HP450 *Love in Pursuit*, D. Mills
___HP454 *Grace in Action*, K. Billerbeck
___HP458 *The Candy Cane Calaboose*, J. Spaeth
___HP461 *Pride and Pumpernickel*, A. Ford
___HP462 *Secrets Within*, G. G. Martin
___HP465 *Talking for Two*, W. E. Brunstetter
___HP466 *Risa's Rainbow*, A. Boeshaar
___HP469 *Beacon of Truth*, P. Griffin
___HP470 *Carolina Pride*, T. Fowler
___HP473 *The Wedding's On*, G. Sattler
___HP474 *You Can't Buy Love*, K. Y'Barbo
___HP477 *Extreme Grace*, T. Davis
___HP478 *Plain and Fancy*, W. E. Brunstetter
___HP481 *Unexpected Delivery*, C. M. Hake
___HP482 *Hand Quilted with Love*, J. Livingston
___HP485 *Ring of Hope*, B. L. Etchison
___HP486 *The Hope Chest*, W. E. Brunstetter
___HP489 *Over Her Head*, G. G. Martin
___HP490 *A Class of Her Own*, J. Thompson
___HP493 *Her Home or Her Heart*, K. Elaine
___HP494 *Mended Wheels*, A. Bell & J. Sagal
___HP497 *Flames of Deceit*, R. Dow & A. Snaden
___HP498 *Charade*, P. Humphrey
___HP501 *The Thrill of the Hunt*, T. H. Murray
___HP502 *Whole in One*, A. Ford

___HP505 *Happily Ever After*, M. Panagiotopoulos
___HP506 *Cords of Love*, L. A. Coleman
___HP509 *His Christmas Angel*, G. Sattler
___HP510 *Past the Ps Please*, Y. Lehman
___HP513 *Licorice Kisses*, D. Mills
___HP514 *Roger's Return*, M. Davis
___HP517 *The Neighborly Thing to Do*, W. E. Brunstetter
___HP518 *For a Father's Love*, J. A. Grote
___HP521 *Be My Valentine*, J. Livingston
___HP522 *Angel's Roost*, J. Spaeth
___HP525 *Game of Pretend*, J. Odell
___HP526 *In Search of Love*, C. Lynxwiler
___HP529 *Major League Dad*, K. Y'Barbo
___HP530 *Joe's Diner*, G. Sattler
___HP533 *On a Clear Day*, Y. Lehman
___HP534 *Term of Love*, M. Pittman Crane
___HP537 *Close Enough to Perfect*, T. Fowler
___HP538 *A Storybook Finish*, L. Bliss
___HP541 *The Summer Girl*, A. Boeshaar
___HP542 *Clowning Around*, W. E. Brunstetter
___HP545 *Love Is Patient*, C. M. Hake
___HP546 *Love Is Kind*, J. Livingston
___HP549 *Patchwork and Politics*, C. Lynxwiler
___HP550 *Woodhaven Acres*, B. Etchison
___HP553 *Bay Island*, B. Loughner
___HP554 *A Donut a Day*, G. Sattler
___HP557 *If You Please*, T. Davis
___HP558 *A Fairy Tale Romance*, M. Panagiotopoulos
___HP561 *Ton's Vow*, K. Cornelius
___HP562 *Family Ties*, J. L. Barton
___HP565 *An Unbreakable Hope*, K. Billerbeck
___HP566 *The Baby Quilt*, J. Livingston
___HP569 *Ageless Love*, L. Bliss
___HP570 *Beguiling Masquerade*, C. G. Page
___HP573 *In a Land Far Far Away*, M. Panagiotopoulos
___HP574 *Lambert's Pride*, L. A. Coleman and R. Hauck

(If ordering from this page, please remember to include it with the order form.)

Presents

Great Inspirational Romance at a Great Price!

Heartsong Presents books are inspirational romances in contemporary and historical settings, designed to give you an enjoyable, spirit-lifting reading experience. You can choose wonderfully written titles from some of today's best authors like Andrea Boeshaar, Wanda E. Brunstetter, Yvonne Lehman, Joyce Livingston, and many others.

When ordering quantities less than twelve, above titles are $2.97 each.
Not all titles may be available at time of order.

SEND TO: **Heartsong Presents** Readers' Service
P.O. Box 721, Uhrichsville, Ohio 44683

Please send me the items checked above. I am enclosing $ _____
(please add $2.00 to cover postage per order. OH add 7% tax. NJ add 6%). Send check or money order, no cash or C.O.D.s, please.

To place a credit card order, call 1-740-922-7280.

NAME _____

ADDRESS _____

CITY/STATE _____ ZIP_____

HP 5-06

♡

HEARTSONG
PRESENTS

If you love Christian romance…

$10.⁹⁹

You'll love Heartsong Presents' inspiring and faith-filled romances by today's very best Christian authors…DiAnn Mills, Wanda E. Brunstetter, and Yvonne Lehman, to mention a few!

When you join Heartsong Presents, you'll enjoy four brand-new, mass market, 176-page books—two contemporary and two historical—that will build you up in your faith when you discover God's role in every relationship you read about!

Mass Market 176 Pages

Imagine…four new romances every four weeks—with men and women like you who long to meet the one God has chosen as the love of their lives…all for the low price of $10.99 postpaid.

To join, simply visit www.heartsong presents.com or complete the coupon below and mail it to the address provided.

✂ -

YES! Sign me up for Hearts♥ng!

NEW MEMBERSHIPS WILL BE SHIPPED IMMEDIATELY!
Send no money now. We'll bill you only $10.99 postpaid with your first shipment of four books. Or for faster action, call 1-740-922-7280.

NAME _____

ADDRESS_____

CITY_____ STATE ـــــ ZIP ـــــ

MAIL TO: HEARTSONG PRESENTS, P.O. Box 721, Uhrichsville, Ohio 44683
or sign up at WWW.HEARTSONGPRESENTS.COM